ISBN: 978-1-7753300-0-4

Thanks to Chris Harrington and Smash the Stigma Canada, Art in House, Robert and Catherine Whone, Neal O'Reilly, Andrew Garfield Mills, and Audrey Jalonen.

Special thanks to Josh Poitras and The Broken Pen Collective for publishing the two poems that appear in this book (*Winter is the Message* and *Phantasmagoria*) in the anthology, *A Blossom in Winter*.

Until you make the unconscious conscious, it will direct your life and you will call it fate.

—*Carl Jung*

THE TW WRATH E LESS E MURDER T THAT PASSES F LOVE O R

Chapter One

Vic didn't have much luck with women until he met Paula. He'd been offered sex by the pimps on Pine Avenue. He had a young woman kiss him for a cab ride after the folk music night, once at a bar. And there was the time he once tried to kiss a woman but she slapped him. He learned to live by himself, loving the lake and the stars and he didn't like coffee much when he was younger, but he began to drink several cups of coffee every day, and eat a bagel and biscuit every morning in his fourteenth year of college.

Paula's bass guitar and laptop computer were stolen by some roommates, thugs looking for a fix. Her sister was an alcoholic that helped Paula move to Toronto from their home-town of Winnipeg, but, looking for something safer, her sister moved north of Toronto. Paula was looking for her first residence in the city where her sister now lived, just north of Toronto. Toronto had become a filthy place in Paula's mind. She had a habit of befriending, under her sister's guidance, the destitute people with addictions and bleak philosophies.

Vic met Paula and her sister on Etherington Crescent, both waiting for the landlord to arrive to show the rooms. The three of them stood at the doorstep smoking cigarettes. Paula didn't say much but her sister spoke on her behalf. They made pleasantries. They hoped the place was nice.

It was the middle of the summer, 2014, and the end of Vic's twelfth year of college.

"That's a nice ring you have, are you close with your dad?" Vic asked. Paula had on a gold ring with the word 'DAD' engraved in it.

"No, not really. I really liked it because I thought it said Dan when I bought it."

"Oh! Who's Dan?" he asked. "Is that your boyfriend?" She didn't respond and Paula's sister looked at Vic surreptitiously, with eyelids gravely swooning to closure. She opened her eyes and gave a bright, crooked smile. He wondered what the gesture of Paula's sister represented. Eventually he would find out.

The landlord arrived and Vic chose the room upstairs almost immediately while Paula didn't speak, her reticence afforded her the musty room in the basement. There was a kitchen upstairs and a kitchen in the basement and on that day they were both tidy. The basement and upstairs were split into two separate, but unlocked apartments.

When they moved in, the front door always stayed unlocked. Paula locked the front door every time she went in and out. The other three roommates, including Vic, didn't care to lock the door. The neighbourhood was safe. Paula had had too many encounters with dangerous people to have felt safe almost anywhere, even in her new home on Lake Simcoe.

Vic was spending his days reading *The Girl with the Dragon Tattoo* on the couch upstairs in the first couple of months they lived on Etherington. Paula would go upstairs and lie down on the couch while Vic read. "Do you read a lot?" she asked, on the third time they were together. He admitted he did, every day. Their togetherness, in those days, was serene and brought them comfort, but conversation was sparse.

Vic had started making an effort to wash his hair and shave his face regularly. He started buying nice used clothes to look good for Paula. He hadn't been habitually cleanly in his pleasant solitude, but as her presence became more common, he learned to keep better care of himself. He was walking home from the used clothing store one summer day when he saw Paula walking toward him, wearing a light shirt that looked painted-on. It made Paula's small breasts more significant. Paula and Vic spoke there, briefly.

"This is the first time I've seen you outside of the house," Vic said.

"Yes, it would be nice to more often," she said.

"We should go for a walk sometime."

They exchanged phone numbers and eventually arranged a time to walk together. Vic had just been released from the hospital for his schizophrenia and was planning to lock himself in his room for a few months. He got caught urinating in a McDonald's parking lot uptown because he hallucinated that someone had moved the McDonald's someplace else. He went looking for the McDonald's to use the men's room but when he didn't see the restaurant in its normal location, and saw no one where the McDonald's usually was, he exposed himself while relieving himself. Of course, everyone who was there was invisible to Vic in his hallucination, but actually a couple of small children saw Vic expose himself. The police saw a video recording of the incident and caught up with Vic to take him to the psychiatric unit at the hospital. He felt no need to tell that story to Paula, despite thinking about it when she asked where he had moved from, but they walked together to the heart of the city in the sun-beating heat of a late July afternoon. As they were downtown, Vic suggested he needed several litres of water to bring home with him. He went into the convenience store and bought two six-litre jugs of distilled water.

"It's hot, but do you really need that much water?" she asked.

"I need the jugs. It's for something." He was planning to use the jugs as urinals for over a month.

She offered to carry one of the jugs when the two of them took the wrong bus home and got lost walking back. Paula became tired and overheated and had to lie down on their search for home. She fell onto someone's lawn in the shade of a tree on one of the passing street corners. *Lay me down in the tall grass and let me do my stuff,* was a line from a Fleetwood Mac song that Vic coincidentally remembered in that moment. Vic sat in front of Paula in the shade.

"This heat is too much," she said. Vic stroked her thigh.

"Is this too much?" he said. She put her arms around his waist.

"We should have some drinks sometime." Paula felt having drinks would appeal to Vic because the men she had known in her past led her to believe that a man's only pastime was drinking alcohol.

"I don't remember the last time I had alcohol," he said, and it pleased her that Vic had spent a long time without alcohol.

They found home. Paula went to her room to rest. She was tired and sweaty from carrying the heavy water jug for several blocks. Vic left his water under the deacon's bench at the door.

PAULA CELEBRATED HER BIRTHDAY with her sister in the middle of August. Paula didn't drink that night but her sister did. Paula complained to her sister about feelings of loneliness, that she hadn't met a new man since she left Toronto. Her sister offered to introduce her to some men, but Paula refused to accept the offer because her sister was an alcoholic and knew primarily other alcoholics. "I'm looking for a certain type," Paula said.

Two days later Victor was having a cigarette on the step outside the front door and Paula was on her way out. "I was thinking I might get some beer on Friday," Vic said. "Sound's good, I'll be here. We can drink in my room," Paula responded. Paula didn't show the apprehension to their arrangement that she truly felt, but she didn't have to travel very far to be close to Vic, and she felt the need to be close to a man, particularly a man whom she admired for spending significantly less time drinking than reading books. Paula at one time in her life had a passion for books and reading.

Late in the afternoon Friday, the day of their date, Vic brought home twelve beers. He thought that might be enough for the both of them. Paula didn't remember they arranged to meet, so Vic knocked on her door around seven o'clock at night. She invited him in but she didn't want any beer. Vic started drinking and they sat together listening to music on the mat she used for a bed. They had in common taciturn personalities. Vic turned up the music when the song *Message in a Bottle* started playing.

"I want to be a writer," Vic said and turned to her, where she lay on the mat.

"Have you always wanted to be a writer?" she asked.

"I wanted to be a doctor first."

"Why didn't you."

"Well, I wasn't so good at school, and they said I was a good singer, and it's a whole convoluted story, and now I want to be a writer. I'll write you letters."

"I guess that's *writing*. I want you to sing for me sometime though."

"I don't love singing anymore, but I will."

"What *do you* love then?"

"I love poetry, the lake, the stars, and..." Vic became pensive, looked at his beer.

"I love the lake too, and the stars," she said.

Vic noticed he had drunk eleven beers. "Here, you keep this last one, I think I should go to bed," he said. It was nearing midnight. "I'll drink with you next time, maybe at the lake," she said. Vic went back upstairs to bed.

When he woke up in the morning he felt a hangover sickness and remembered that he didn't like alcohol very much. He went out to the front step for a cigarette then went back to bed until the afternoon. Vic didn't read that day. There weren't any lights in the living room and by the time he felt like reading, the sun had already gone down. Vic was disappointed.

Paula woke up around noon, and noticed the beer Vic had left in her room. She ostensibly heard the guy that lived in the room next to her yelling at her and mocking her. She picked up the beer and hid it in the back of her closet. Her closet had no door, but there was a pile of dirty clothes where the door was supposed to be. She noticed stains of excrement on several pairs of panties lying in the pile. She had the thought to wash her dirty laundry but she just lay back down on her mat and turned on the television.

Paula watched television religiously. She watched funny shows, cooking shows, home remodeling shows, interior design shows, but her favourites were the horror movies late at night and any kind of documentary about The Doors or Jim Morrison. For about an hour she watched television then went upstairs to the doorstep for a cigarette. *Another bitch-stick,* she thought.

She was glad Vic wasn't around, but then the roommate from the room beside her walked up to the driveway carrying a bag and eating a coconut chocolate bar he had just bought from the dollar store several kilometers away. "Nice day," he said as he walked past her on his way into the house. Paula barely noticed his presence. She was deep in thought, and after he went inside she realized someone had been there, and recalled his words. "Ya," she replied.

Paula had bleached blonde hair, grey eyes, stood just over five feet tall, weighed a hundred pounds, ate sparingly, and thought nothing of skipping breakfast, lunch and dinner on most days. She didn't have much money for food, let alone money for the overpriced long, slim cigarettes she found aesthetically pleasing to smoke. She went inside and continued watching television shows. A rerun of *Family Feud* was supposed to be starting in five minutes.

Before Vic went to bed he went out for his last cigarette of the day. He noticed in the ashtray on the step that Paula's slim cigarettes had been discarded there. The mark of her presence satisfied him. He finished his cigarette and went inside to sleep.

In the morning he was excited that he had a chance to finally read again. He waited patiently, building the excitement of seeing her again, until the sunlight came though the large picture window in the living room. *The Girl with the Dragon Tattoo* was there on the end table when he curled up on the couch to read. The air conditioning in the house was perfect and he planned to go out for a walk later in the day.

Paula came upstairs and curled up on the other end of the couch while Victor read his book. The feeling of her presence elevated the pleasure of his reading. They didn't speak. They didn't say hello or goodbye. Vic finished three relatively long chapters by the time the day had turned to dusk then he slowly got up, trying not to disrupt Paula's peacefulness, leaving to go for a walk before making supper. He grabbed his phone, went out to the doorstep, plugged in his earphones, lit a cigarette, and went for a walk. He walked to the lake to find a good spot to take Paula.

Chapter Two

On his way back from the lake, Vic stopped at a little plaza near the beer store. He went into the little convenience store that was run by an old Chinese couple, and their grown-up children. There was an old man buying lottery tickets in front of Vic in line. The old man was rummaging through his bill fold and pockets looking for exact change.

"Excuse me sir," Vic said, "You have a thing in your hair." The man had a neatly trimmed hair cut with a small bit from a coniferous tree dangling from his hair. The man turned around.

"Pardon me?" he said.

"You have some pine needles in your hair," Vic said as the old man slowly made cognizance of the statement. The old man reached for his hair languidly, finding the needles then examined them in his hand. The man said something incomprehensible, like he was trying to make a joke, but his wit failed him in that moment. The old man turned back around and dumped a bunch of change and a five dollar bill onto the counter.

"I'm not sure if this is correct, have a look," the old man said. The young, Chinese woman at the counter approved of his change. "Uh huh," she said. "Are you happy," the old man asked. She looked at Vic and smiled, denoting the cuteness of the man's senility. "Yes, I'm happy," she said.

Vic noticed that she was pregnant. He was glad she told the old man she was happy because he had imagined how much trouble it would be for him to have a child, supporting a family, on the very little income he had. He stepped up to the counter to pay for his cola.

"Dollar twenty-five," she said.

"Oh, you've raised the prices," Vic responded. He only had a dollar.

"Yes, since last week, sorry."

Vic began towards the door. The old man was slowly putting away the things he had emptied out of his wallet and dropped a receipt on the floor. He was blocking the doorway. Vic picked up the receipt and handed it to the man.

"Oh, everything's happening to me today," the man said.

"You're fine."

The man let Vic out the door, and Vic sat on the curb and lit a cigarette. A few minutes later the old man walked slowly by Vic and handed him a two-dollar coin. "Have a nice day," he said to Vic. Vic thanked him, got up and walked home. It was the last three dollars Vic would have for another two weeks, until his cheque from the government came on the thirty-first of August, so he decided to save it in case something came up.

Paula went out to the step for a cigarette before she went to bed. It was dark out but there was a dim light in the awning above the step, attracting moths and flies. She felt a couple drops of rain coming down and within a few moments it began to pour down. She heard Vic's quick, splashing steps as he ran towards the door. "Just made it," he said "Whew!"

She asked where he went, and he told her the story of the old man in the convenience store. He told her he was extremely happy to have tripled his spending power. Then he took out his pack of cigarettes and noticed he only had four left. Paula offered him one. "I've only got twenty dollars until my cheque comes," she said, "I can probably afford one more pack."

Paula didn't smoke as heavily as Vic, but Vic had other methods to keep up his habit. They each smoked a cigarette, remaining silent for a few minutes. "It's nice standing so close to the pouring rain, without actually getting wet. It's ferocious but calming at the same time," he said. She didn't respond but the two of them stood there in admiration of the rain, smoking. Vic finished his cigarette and excused himself on account of his wet clothes, saying goodnight to Paula.

In the morning, Vic was careful not to smoke more than one cigarette on the step. He held that two-dollar coin between his fingers, admiring it. He wasn't quite sure what to do with it, at first. He decided to walk to the corner to get a donut smoking his second cigarette on the way and noticed a woman coming out from the path of the park, onto the street right in front of him.

She looked over at Vic and waved her hand at him. He thought she was beautiful. She was wearing leather sandals and a short t-shirt that showed her midriff. He struggled to take his eyes off her tummy as she asked him for a cigarette.

He was apprehensive about giving her one when he noticed he only had two left.

"I've only got two, but you can have one because I think you're pretty."

"Oh, you're sweet," she said, "Hey, I'm going for breakfast, why don't you come with me?" she said.

"Okay, sure."

Vic was ecstatic about meeting this young lady, but still felt a little uneasy. She had a very outgoing personality, and she talked a lot. She talked about several of her friends while she was out with Vic at the diner. She ordered a bagel, biscuit and coffee. Vic just ordered a coffee to go, because he anxiously felt she might find him disagreeable and that she would request for him to leave. But as they talked, although Vic mainly listened to her, she felt comfortable around him. She was debating by herself about her next move regarding the friends she discussed. She resolved to believe that her friends did not exist unless they were present, in wondering whether they thought of her when she was not there. Therefore, their non-existence made all of her thoughts of them extraneous. He told her the notion was brilliant. It seemed to Vic that she was caught up in feeling a little neglected by someone in particular, but she avoided any specific details, and he felt it wasn't any of his business to pry.

She thought he was cute in a quirky way, in that he was apprehensive to say almost anything, and she was pleased that he didn't stare at her body. He avoided looking at her body because he found her extremely attractive, and didn't want to feel guilty about seeing her through that filter. He made eye-contact quite frequently instead and to her this showed he was very engaged. As their conversations ended, she was contented that she had asked him to come along.

They went to the cash after she finished her breakfast, paid, and then she told him she was buying a pack of cigarettes. She had just quit smoking but wanted to pay him back for the cigarette. She went into the convenience store then came out unravelling the plastic wrap on the package of cigarettes. She opened the pack, and offered Vic a couple.

"Thanks," he said, taking two.

"Let's do this again," she said, "you're sweet."

"I like you to," he said. "Okay!"

"Here, take my number. My name's Sarah, text me." He nervously punched in her number into his phone.

"I'll see you around."

"I'm off to work now. Have a nice day. Hope to hear from you soon," she said and walked towards where all the buses stop, on their trips uptown and downtown. Vic went back home, elated.

When he got home he went to his room and picked up his notebook and a pen and lay down on his bed. He began writing a poem about his experience finding a spot at the lake, the old man, the two-dollar coin, his two dollar coffee with Sarah, and the free cigarette. He was absorbed into writing, until he noticed the time. As he was writing it, he remembered he had a class on Tuesday at noon, and he had less than thirty minutes to get there. He put down his pen and notebook, got ready to leave with his things, and ran to the college, not quite finished his poem.

When he got to the class he was fifteen minutes late but the teacher didn't notice Vic had arrived and didn't give him the assignment. Mr. McNeil began talking about the assignment and Vic had to mention that he didn't have the assignment papers yet.

Mr. McNeil told him he should probably come to class on time to keep up with the assignments and the content of the class. Vic went up to the teacher's desk to get the handout then Mr. McNeil started his lecture for the day. Afterwards, the teacher began to speak of the assignment he had handed out at the beginning of class. Vic got lost near the end of the document, not noticing there was another page on the assignment hand-out. Vic mumbled to himself, "I think you forgot something."

"What's that, Victor?" Mr. McNeil said.

"You're missing a page. You keep going, but none of this, that date, isn't written anywhere on the hand-out." Vic explained.

"Not at all."

The teacher stormed out towards Vic's seat, snatched the sheet of paper out of Vic's hand in a dour manner, put his finger on his tongue and flipped the sheet out from where it had been sticking together. He slapped it on Vic's desk, pulled the pen out of his breast pocket and circled the exact date he had referred to in his lecture.

Vic was furious. He got up out of his seat, shoved the sheet of paper into his bag, walked out of the class, and flashed the teacher his middle finger through the window of the door. "It better be done next week, or you've had the biscuit," Mr. McNeil said, not noticing Vic's lewd gesture.

Vic walked home. *Everyone hates me. I'm useless, and people treat me like a huge loser*, he thought, unable to remove his thoughts of self-loathing from his head. Paula was on the step having a cigarette when Vic arrived home but he just walked by her into the house. He lay on his bed, picked up his notebook and tried to read his poem but was unable to concentrate. He felt his poem was a useless waste of ink, as useless as he felt he was to others, or useless as anything he may have done with himself. He ripped the poem out of the notebook and ripped the page into tiny pieces and dropped them onto his bed.

He paused for a while and struggled to stop his quick breathing. While focusing on his breathing, eventually it slowed down to a natural pace. He went back to the step for a cigarette when he started to feel calmer. Paula had already gone back in to start doing her laundry. He remembered at breakfast Sarah said, "If they aren't around, they don't exist," to relieve the stresses of thinking of others when they weren't around. Victor lit up a cigarette, smoked it and felt better. *Mr. McNeil doesn't exist*, he thought. The thought that his teacher had disappeared from his imagination satisfied him. He went inside and began research on his assignment, and started writing his findings after dinner.

She had been nervous that the noise of the laundry machines would upset the roommates when she fell asleep with her last load of laundry in the dryer. She had become paranoid that the other roommates thought she was loud but actually she made hardly any noise at all. Sleeping was her best coping mechanism to the loudness of her mind. She spent so much time in a vegetative state—sleeping, watching television, avoiding most physical activities—her consequently scant energy levels made her mind more overactive to compensate.

One of the reasons she moved to the neighbourhood of

Etherington Crescent was because the college was nearby. She intended to get a certificate at the college, which would be paid for as part of the social assistance she received. To enroll in classes at the college in the fall, she had a small stack of paperwork to be filled out in the top drawer of her dresser. Returning to college was an amendment to her first failed attempt at college—for a time, she tried her hand at studying to be a librarian when she lived in Toronto.

She was a librarian's assistant at a high school library as a college placement internship. During her placement she was asked to suggest a collection of books for the library. All of the interns had to display their new collections before the books would be shelved. Paula had thought of all of the literature that had become movies, so her idea was to compile a collection of books that were novelized from their original movie versions.

When her collection was unveiled, her co-workers kindly thanked her for the collection, but behind her back, they dismissed her collection as lacking any literary sophistication. She felt ostracized by them and became insecure around her coworkers for the year remaining of her internship. After that, she struggled in her program and became unsure that she was meant to be there, like she was an imposter.

In the morning, Vic went to the laundry room to check if the machines were available. He opened the dryer and he noticed it was full of clothes. He pulled out a few pieces of clothing to see who they belonged to. As he put the clothes back in the dryer, a tiny pair of panties fell on the concrete floor. He knew it belonged to Paula. He was amazed by the size of the underwear. He hadn't noticed how small she was until that moment.

He pulled down his pants and briefs and shook them out from around his feet. He took Paula's pair of underwear and tried to put them on. They wouldn't fit over his thighs and began stretching when he got them past his knees. He took them off, hoping Paula wouldn't notice he had stretched them slightly, and threw them back in the dryer. He put his clothes back on and looked towards the door.

He saw that no one was watching, so he went upstairs and out onto the doorstep for a cigarette. His assignment was almost finished, but he had all week to complete it. He had no other obligations that week. The only class he had selected for the semester allowed him to continue progressing through college at a snail's pace. He felt like seeing Sarah, but he had only one dollar, so he spent the rest of the afternoon reading *The Girl with the Dragon Tattoo* on the couch when the sun was shining through the living room window, and went for a walk in the evening.

When Paula woke up she took her clothes out of the dryer. Again she worried that she had caused too much noise, that one of the roommates was inconvenienced because she left the machine to run overnight. In fact, Vic was happy about it, living in the room directly above the laundry room. It reminded him that he had to do his own laundry. She folded her clothes and put them away. Only her underwear and bras remained on her mat. She hung up her bras and picked up the underwear then put them in her top drawer. She took her college application papers out of the top drawer first to make room for her clean underwear.

In the afternoon she filled out the papers and brought them into the registrar's office at the college, one block away from

Etherington Crescent. She felt great that day. She went to the diner on the corner for a roast beef sandwich. It was the best dinner she had had all summer, and she was completely satisfied, yet resultedly out of money.

She went to curl up on the couch next to Vic the next day while he read his book. They didn't speak but both of them enjoyed the company of one another. Vic went out to the doorstep and smoked a few of Paula's discarded slim cigarettes after he finished reading two long chapters. When he came back inside Paula had stretched out and fallen asleep. He went to his room to lie down, but he wasn't tired. He went for a walk after dusk when the heat had fallen to a nice cool temperature, perfect for walking.

By the end of August, the air conditioning in the house stopped working, and there was a delay in having it repaired by the landlord. The weather was quite hot during that time. It was duly noticed when Paula came to relax while Vic read his book, but it was because of the broken air conditioner and the almost unbearable, humid, late-August heat that they finally made some headway in the relationship.

Chapter Three

Vic began having difficulty reading his book while Paula was curled up on the couch next to him. He struggled to take his mind off of her presence. She wasn't an annoyance, it was just the opposite. A few times when she joined him while he read in late August, the air conditioner was still in need of repair and there seemed to be a final summer heatwave going through the city.

She lay on the couch, taking up much less than half the space Vic took up with his six-foot-five, two-hundred pound frame. He held his book up to his face, not reading, leaving a window of space for a line of sight at Paula. He stared and felt a great pleasure in their togetherness. He became overwhelmed by a feeling of nothingness—a sweet sum of everything they befell into together, free of tangibility, or propriety—causing him to feel sheer pleasure. His thoughts became threats against this great pleasure, and in hopes of prolonging the feeling, like delaying the climax of his Zen, he focused deeply, more passionately on her physical being in a sidelong disinterest. The pleasure was the ability of her to be being at his side, in that moment, free of entity, and he felt they were together in losing everything, giving everything to an infinity of nothing, yet receiving so much. But his Zen soon vanished.

She spoke.

"How old are you?" she asked. She hardly spoke, but this time she startled him. She had been wondering the likelihood that he'd be too overwhelmed by her nudity. She felt a great satisfaction in his taciturn, reticent, openness to communal silence. He told her he was thirty-one years old. She assumed he had experienced many loves with women, by that age. Vic was an attractive man, and she felt he exuded a silent confidence. She felt she wouldn't offend him as a man of experience, so she took off her shirt. "The shirt was sticking to my skin, it's so humid. Pray there's a breeze," she said.

His Zen vanished.

She revealed a tattoo on her shoulder of a large blossom, with her bra strap covering only a strip of the flower, and a large scar on her stomach looking like a remnant of an abandoned train track. "What's that scar on your stomach," he asked.

"Oh, that's the first thing you notice? Did you see the tattoo?" she said.

"I'm sorry, I saw the tattoo. It's pretty."

"Well, it's from a man. He was evil. In ninety-seven … no … ninety-eight … I can't remember. It was New Year's Eve. He loved me, but I was engaged to his partner. He couldn't have me."

He paused for a moment, expecting more to the story. "Is that the story of the tattoo or the scar?" he asked.

"I'm a liar. No one has ever, in all of history, wanted to hear the truth. Honesty is a mark of ignorance," she said.

"So you're saying philosophy is a four-letter word?"

"Not philosophy—truth,"

"I suppose that's an interesting way to put it. *Honestly...* I feel better when you're here. I hope you know that."

"Well, I'm sorry it's just a flower. I didn't know dragon tattoos would be so popular in 2014. If you like me around so much, let's go out Saturday night. We both get our cheques tomorrow then we can go down to the lake on Saturday. I'll drink with you this time. I think we said we would, right?"

"Thy will be done. T'will be so fun," he said, confirming in exuberance.

She invited him into the basement where it was cooler. She left her shirt on the couch when they went to her room. She took her key out and unlocked her door, although she struggled for a minute to find the correct key. She shivered as she walked in her room, "oooooh," she said, interjecting her quiver.

"See I told you it was cooler in here," she said. She went to her closet, to the hiding spot where she placed Vic's beer. "Remember this?" she asked.

"My hands are cold, feel them," she said as she lay on the mat. Vic opened his beer and sat on her mat, drinking it. He reached for her hand. To him, her hand felt atrophied, lifeless, and lacked any kind of dexterity. He found her hands quite unattractive because of this, yet they were cold. He went back upstairs to get her shirt.

By the time he came back to give her the t-shirt, she had placed herself underneath the heavy, black, woven duvet. He noticed she had taken off her pants and they were left aside the mat, so he dropped the shirt next to them.

"I'm naked and ready for bed now," she said.

"Okay goodnight," he said. He picked up his can of beer and went upstairs onto the step just outside the front door and smoked a couple of the unfinished cigarettes he scavenged from the smoking area at the college that morning. It was only a quarter-to-seven, so he finished his beer and went for a walk.

Paula woke up before dawn excited that she would have a large amount of money (by her standards) in the morning and was looking forward to going to the diner for breakfast. Just after midnight she watched the end of a suspenseful sci-fi movie and went back to sleep. She woke up in the morning and looked in the mail box for her cheque. She made note of Vic's last name on his mail. She was fascinated by the name Glatt. She wondered the heritage. She was a Scandinavian descended Hansen, from her Father's side, and an Irish McVey on her Mother's. She suspected Glatt may have been of Scandinavian descent.

She went to the bank on the corner and deposited her cheque in the morning and went almost right next-door to the diner to have French toast and extra sausage and eggs. Vic didn't run into her but he did almost the same thing that morning, although he didn't make it to the diner. He went to the bank to deposit his cheque. However, the first thing he thought when he woke up was that Paula might have tried to seduce him. He became anxious that Paula might have felt insulted, that she thought he was insecure or even worse, that he wasn't attracted to her.

He had an odd experience with the bank teller as a result of this anxiety. He felt his bank card password had been compromised, so he asked the teller for a new bank card. She took him to the automated teller machine to show him how to create a new password. Anxious, because the female teller was looking over his shoulder, he created the new password rather haphazardly, and within minutes he wasn't sure he remembered the number. He then withdrew seventy-five dollars with the female teller, and as she withdrew it from the till, she dropped the five-dollar bill onto the floor. She was confident she had in her hands the correct amount, and forgot how much money was requested as she doled out the bills. "Sixty," she said, quickly resolving to the final, "and seventy," as she ostensibly completed the task of handing the money over, placing the penultimate bill on the counter.

Victor became furious.

"Are you trying to steal five dollars from me?" he accused.

"Sorry?" she honestly asked.

"I requested seventy-five dollars," he said "you're trying to steal five dollars from me! You know, I don't have very much money. I'm a poor man. How dare you?" She looked at the ground where the bill had fallen. She picked it up and showed it to Vic.

"I just dropped it on the floor. I knew I withdrew the correct amount—my mistake."

"Okay," he said, "you need to be more careful because I don't have five dollars to waste."

"My apologies Mr. Glatt, but you would have certainly had that money deposited back in your account by the end of the day. It's no cause for worry," she said.

"Okay, fine, I'm just glad I got it. Have a nice day."

"You too. My apologies."

Vic was upset by the bank teller, and couldn't get the thought of Paula's seduction off of his mind. He was worried he wasted his chance with Paula. As he walked out of the bank, he realized he had the seventy-five dollars in his hand. He became worried that someone would see him holding it, so he quickly placed the money into his pocket and forgot about it. Then he went next-door to the pharmacy. *It's one or the other*, he thought.

He grabbed a four-litre jug of bleach from the back. Then he became even more anxious as he was looking at the condoms. He picked out a package of condoms from the shelf and went to the back of the store where the pharmacist took payments for medication, where he wouldn't have to wait in line or be seen by other customers. He forgot that he had cash, and when the pharmacist rang up the price for the jug of bleach and box of condoms, he decided to pay with his debit card. He put the card in and couldn't get the password right.

He was becoming more frustrated with the scenario. Finally he remembered that he had a new card given to him that morning which rectified the correct password in his mind. "It's not my card. I forgot what she told me the password was," he explained, lying to her, excusing his bemusement.

The payment went through. Vic picked up the jug of bleach off of the counter. He asked the pharmacist to place the condoms in a bag because he didn't want to display them as he walked home. The pharmacist sort of giggled because he had convinced her that some woman was hot for him and gave him money to buy condoms, but Vic felt condescended by the pharmacist's snicker. He wasn't in a state to interpret her endearing gesture.

The pharmacist placed the condoms in a paper bag and Vic walked home with the condoms and jug, not sure which purchase would get used. He left the bleach in his closet, and opened the box of ten condoms and dumped the two little gold strips, five condoms per strip, into the top drawer of his bedside table. He was curious about how to put one on. He ripped one apart from one of the strips and looked at it, pleased to have them in his possession, then put the condom in his pocket. He went to the kitchen and toasted some bread, placed some shaved chicken on it and ate the sandwich and then some cookies.

Vic felt better once he had eaten breakfast. He noticed Paula going to the doorstep for a cigarette a few minutes later. His anxiety diffused completely, seeing her, but he realized he forgot to buy a pack of cigarettes. He went outside to join her. She gave him a cigarette and told him about the sci-fi movie, and her big breakfast. She was having a great day and her spirit enlivened him. After that she told him she was looking forward to Saturday night with him. He was surprised—she didn't remember they had arranged a date the first time they had one.

He remembered the perfect spot he found at the lake. He didn't tell her where he was taking her, but when she went inside he worried how much beer to buy her. She didn't seem to drink much the first time, and twelve was far too much for just him. His thoughts misguided him again in a slight discord. He felt pleasant in her presence, but because of that he felt awful when she was away.

Chapter Four

The next morning Vic woke up in his room with clothes strewn about and noticed the unpacked boxes. He put his house pants on, picked up his laundry and put it on his bed. He opened one of the boxes and started placing his books onto the shelves. He did the same with the next box. In the third box were his turntable, stereo receiver, cables and small speakers. He had a small table where he set up his stereo. The last box he opened contained a small vinyl record collection of about seventy albums. He placed them on the leftover space on his shelves with the books and some of his clothes. He took his laundry and threw it into the big empty box that had contained the stereo components.

He flipped through his records to choose one. His room was looking tidy when the boxes were placed in his large, walk-in closet. He went to the hall closet for the vacuum cleaner to get rid of the poem he had ripped into confetti almost two weeks prior. His room was finally looking charming. Then he remembered his condom. He rummaged through his laundry for the condom he left in his pocket and placed it on top of his bedside table.

Proud of his dapper room, he made his bed and lay in it listening to the The Beatles' *The White Album*, pondering the conspicuous condom. His thoughts began to fluctuate between great happiness and severe anxiety, regarding the visible condom.

In the afternoon he walked to the liquor store downtown and forgot that the condom remained visible by his bedside. As he walked to the liquor store he worried about what to buy, but when he got there the huge selection of spirits pleased him and he selected something almost immediately. He was satisfied buying his twelve bottles of beer and by the time he arrived back to his room he had completely forgotten the condom was there, let alone noticing it.

He tried to read in the living room in the afternoon while the sun was shining through the picture window but he was unable to focus on the book, excited to see Paula in the evening. She spent the day watching television after she showered and ate breakfast. She tried to toast a piece of bread but the overflowing crumbs in the tray at the bottom of the toaster prevented it from working so she made a peanut butter and jam sandwich.

All of the plates in the downstairs kitchen were left in the sink like the housemates were waiting for the maid to show up sometime soon. Of course, there was no maid and the plates remained there. Each plate was cleaned and used one meal at a time, thereafter. Paula used serviettes instead of a plate. She didn't really know how to prepare much other than toast, and even if she did, she didn't eat regularly enough to make use of her groceries before they perished.

And then the time of night came that Vic went downstairs and knocked on her door. "Are you ready?" he said. She opened her door slightly and he wasn't sure he was supposed to enter, but he watched her put on makeup through the crack. She went behind the door for a couple of minutes then came out of her room. She was wearing a two-tone white dress with a see-through, eggshell-coloured, pleated material below the waist that had an attached white slip underneath. The dress had short sleeves, was tight against her waist and bust, but puffed out around her hips. She had on an argyle fedora and green New Balance running shoes. Vic slightly noticed her attire, but was attracted to her eye-colour. She had on contact lenses that made her eye-colour blue. "Are you ready?" she said.

He picked up his backpack with the case of beers in it, and they began walking to the lake. It was two-and-a-half kilometers to the lake. Paula became tired only a short distance from Etherington. He asked her if he could sing for her. She remembered she told him she wanted to hear him sing and became excited about the idea.

He tried singing *Blackbird* but he couldn't remember all of the words. He felt embarrassed for a moment then he quickly resolved to sing a song which he felt was just as apropos. He started singing the first verse of *Dear Prudence*, by The Beatles. By the time the next verse came around Paula began singing along. She continued to sing with him the rest, following his lead.

"Dear Prudence! The wind is low, the birds will sing that you are part of everything …" they sang boisterously.

They were arriving at a small park that overlooked the

lake from about two-hundred feet above, and Vic felt joyous in their togetherness, singing with Paula. The sunset behind them lit the whole horizon over the lake, pink and orange.

The sweetness of the sky, lighting the clouds like pink cotton candy, ignited Vic. "Wait … Wait … How about this one?" he said as they sauntered down the staircase, from the top of the lookout, adjoined in a blissful rhythmic lilt. "Why don't we d-do it in the road?" he began singing. "Why don't we do it in the road?" he continued. He sensed a glare of disapproval from Paula. She wasn't familiar with that song by The Beatles, and hardly knew any of the songs from *The White Album*. Vic meant it as a joke.

"No," she said emphatically, "stop it now." He had already stopped singing, noticing her furrowed brow. In a spontaneous quip he interjected her disapproval—"Cre-e-e-am tangerine… an' monde allais mal"—creating a French pun by replacing the word Montelimar from The Beatles' song *Savoy Truffle*— attempting to display his wit only to baffle hers. Then a timely concentrating silence came over them as he led her, carefully tiptoeing, down the steep embankment of the lake.

They had arrived. "It's wonderful," he sighed.

The rising moon leaned into the tail end of the crepuscule like a satisfied lover. He put his backpack down and pulled two bottles of beer out of it. She took the beer when he handed it to her. They were both surprised she took it, but she struggled to open the cap. He opened it for her and they were both surprised again when she took it back and surprised once more when she finally took a sip.

"It *is* a cream tangerine—the sky tonight," she remarked. She was pleased by the scenery, but she was too delighted about the opportunity to reveal her good news to be vexed by Vic's inscrutable wit. "There's a perfect spot to sit over here," he suggested, showing her some large rocks with flat edges on top. They moved to the seats and as time passed a couple of stars bagan to shine through the marble of billows and sky. Vic lit a cigarette, so she did too.

"So I noticed your name on your mail—Glatt, is that Scandinavian?" she asked.

"I don't really know. It's my Father's name, and he doesn't speak of his past. His life begins and ends in a successful career with no rise to his position. He has no story. A person with no story is like a man with no name, almost inhuman."

"Sometimes people are afraid of their story and where they came from. I am sometimes."

"Everyone is. The whole world is a crack in a sidewalk that's been pounded on by the feet of generations and generations, and we're all just trying to live and grow out of it. Our story is all we have to share. There's nothing in life worth more. I remember the days that shined and the days I got rained on, and maybe not everyone is ready to hear it, but if you really care about someone, shouldn't you give them the only thing that you have that has a value?"

She hadn't realized how challenging Vic would be, wishing she could impart a snippet of her past but they drank their beers, silenced by his rhetorical question. A few moments of silence passed by. "Suffice it to say that I'm Canadian and that's all of my heritage that I'm allowed to know," he said, removing the paperweight to throw it into the lake, freeing his story to blow away into the wind.

"Do you like Canada? Are you proud to be Canadian?"

"Well, I like Wayne Gretzky," he said and she laughed.

"A toast ... to Wayne Gretzky!"

They drank beer, and she pulled him into the story of her first experience going to college. She omitted the part about the mental illness she suffered as her academic life failed, leading her into a life of alcoholism with her sister in Toronto and the drug-addicted, boozy men that were around, euphemizing that, *college wasn't right for me at that time in my life.* And she turned the subject to her recent registration at the college and that her intention for moving into their house on Etherington Crescent was to be close enough to the college to try again.

Vic was excited at the idea. He spoke about the value of being in college and that he had failed repeatedly, almost habitually, throughout his twelve years there, omitting that his failures were because of his recurring stays at the local mental hospital. He suggested that her presence around the campus in the fall would be inspiring to him. They drank more, celebrating her good news.

They smoked cigarettes and drank each bottle of beer joyfully, each one more joyful than the last and hardly noticed that the marble sky had congealed into an overcast lens over the entire sky and moon—the moon adding only a dull light to the lights of the city that shined from across the lake.

"Last one ... say something philosophical," he said, removing the last two bottles from his bag.

"Something philosophical," she replied. She hearkened his laughter for approval of her humour, and as he laughed heartily, so did she.

"Atta-girl!" he said as she took a swig.

"Oh?" she said inquisitively and reached out her hand as a light mist began falling, "What do we have here?" They both looked at the sky.

The mist was heated like a morning in late May and the sky was pleasant but overcast over the calm lake. "This could get bad," he said. She got up, carrying her beer, and went toward the dirt platform at the bottom of the embankment. "Who cares? Come here," she said. She took her phone out of her purse, started playing a song, and turned the volume all the way up. She propped up her fedora on a rock and placed her phone underneath. "Dance with me," she said.

The song began with a sound-clip of a thundering rain-storm. "I hope this isn't going to turn into that kind of storm," he said, listening to the recording play, clearly, as the hat covered her phone from the falling mist, amplifying the sound. The recording transitioned into a moody bass line at the pace of a quick walk. He placed his bottle down, and awkwardly took hold of Paula, leading her at the tempo. Atop the bass line, the Fender Rhodes placidly pitter-pattered with a sweetly descending melody.

It was the most beautiful thing Vic ever felt, and when she said, "no, slowly," it didn't upset him that he felt naive. "I've never danced with a woman before," he said, took her at half the tempo, and it was even more amorous that way. "Riders on the storm," Jim Morrison sang, "Riders on the storm."

So slowly, the pace of their dance was more tiresome than the actual tempo, yet the mist falling was energizing. As the moody song developed, so did a slight rainfall. "We should go, but this feels perfect," he said. She whispered for him to shush and the rain began to swell denser until the music from the phone speaker couldn't be heard by the end of the song. "We better go before the hill gets muddy," he said. He went back to the rocks, placed the empty bottles in his bag while Paula gathered her hat and phone, then he quickly led the way back up towards the lookout.

They drunkenly ran across the road to the steps that went up to the lookout. The rainfall had collected into small pools which they splashed with their feet as they jogged up the stairs. The rain fell hard and warm. Paula struggled to jog all the way up to the lookout because her dress had adhered to her legs and when Vic arrived at the top, he turned around and waited for Paula. Slowly she arrived at the top and he cheered her arrival. Paula held out her hands to hug him, but he grabbed both of her hands and raised them over her head, pulling her body against his waist. "Wooooo-ooooh!" he screamed. They laughed.

He held onto her hand and led her in a quick walk back towards Etherington. They sang, repeating, "Riders on the storm!" loudly until the rain stopped and they slowed their walking pace—their soaking wet clothes like elastic bands wrapped around their bodies. Vic let go of Paula's hand—when the rain stopped, he felt like their undercover had been exposed, and Paula felt like she had just climbed out of a toilet bowl.

Under the tin awning at the front door they both lit cigarettes. "It's been swell," Vic said, looking at Paula hoping they would kiss. There was a flying beetle smacking itself over and over into the light in the awning and it disgusted Paula "I've gotta get outta here and outta these clothes. I gotta lie down," she said, "I'll see you again shortly," and went back inside, into her room.

Vic swatted at the beetle for a few minutes, trying to stop it from crashing into the light. He knocked it down but he didn't see where it went. He sat down on the dry stoop and lit another cigarette. He thought of the night with Paula. He was completely satisfied by her—it—there was nothing ever any better. He put out his cigarette in the ashtray and noticed the beetle was stuck, lodged into a crack in the wooden planks of the stoop. He didn't want to touch it, so he looked for a twig on the lawn to poke it out of the crack. The beetle was in there so tightly it couldn't even squirm and he spent a half-hour trying to dislodge it.

Chapter Five

After Vic dislodged the flying beetle he went upstairs to his room, put on a Lou Reed vinyl record and fell asleep before the side was over. Paula had changed into a short, tight shirt and underwear and was lying under her black duvet with one leg uncovered. She had expected Vic to come downstairs to see her. An hour after she left him, she supposed he had went to bed but she felt disappointed. The roommate in the room next to hers began to take over her thoughts. She still was under the assumption that he found her to be noisy. It wasn't the case at all. Paula hardly ever made a noise.

Vic was disrupted from his sleep just after three o'clock in the morning. He didn't know what all the commotion was. The other roommates knew exactly what it was—that's why they didn't go to the door to attempt to stop it. Vic had to use the toilet anyway, so he furtively crept down the hallway so as to not startle the aggravated person at the door. He heard the door slamming over and over. As Vic got closer to the end of the hall, scared, he realized it was Paula creating the commotion.

"You think I make noise?" she shouted, "How's this for noise?" she continued—SLAM! —The door slammed shut and then the door creaked as she opened it again. "The land-lord says I can use the kitchen. I have every right to use the dishes, I don't know why you keep trying to stop me," she shouted, "Ahoo, ahooo," she cried.

Vic wondered who she was talking to. He took a peek around the end of the hallway to look at Paula at the front door. It was dark in the living room but the light on the land-ing was lit. SLAM! —She went back outside angrily.

Vic waited at the top of the steps for a minute, peeked at Paula to see if she was with anyone and wanted to get a better read on her condition. "I don't know why you give me such a hard time about the noise. I can barely hear the television. Do you want me to watch the goddamn thing with no sound at all?" she said and started crying some more. "Ahooo-ooo! Ahoo-ahoo!" As if someone was replying to her questions she retorted, "I pay my rent. You don't have any right to tell me to leave. This is my house!"

Vic was baffled. She was shouting and making enough noise to alarm the neighbours and have the police sent to the house. He began to infiltrate the commotion by walking over to the landing by the door. "Oh, what do you want?" Paula said. Vic didn't say anything. He grabbed Paula's hand and she jerked it away from him. She went back outside and slammed the door behind her.

Vic opened the door as Paula stood there looking down to the ground. "Ahooo-ahoo, ahoo-ahoo-ahoo, ahoo-hoo," she sobbed. He grabbed her shoulders and pulled her into his body and hugged her. He held her very tight. She sobbed at great length, making a muffled sound with her face pressed against his chest. She became calm when Vic soothed her. "shhh ... shhhhh-shhhhh ... it's okay," he gently repeated to her.

She pulled her face away from his chest, gasping for air, and a string of saliva dangled between his chest and her mouth. Then she slammed her face into his chest and bellowed, "Eeeeyyyyuuugggghhhh!"

"It's okay ... It's okay ... Everything's fine ... What's wrong girl?" he asked.

"It's you. Why do you do it to me?" she asked.

"What did I do? I thought we had a great night."

"So why didn't you come see me? I always come see you. Where are you? You never come see me. I just wish you were there for me," she said and slammed her face into his chest. "ahooooo-oooo, ahoo-ahoo-ahoo," she cried.

"It's okay sweetie, I'm here. I came to see you. I want to see you. I'll come see you," he said, seeming insincere to her.

"Ugggggghhhh!"

"I mean that. I'll come see you every day. I swear I really didn't know you wanted me around."

"I want you to come to my room right now. I want you to fuck me."

Vic felt a pang of emotions in that moment. He held hands with a little girl when he was seven years old. Her brother married the two of them in Vic's driveway a few months after that. She told Vic he sounded like a frog when he said "I do." His seven year old wife's comments made him anxious and insecure, so he ran away and they didn't speak for weeks after, and they didn't keep in touch after he moved away the following summer. The last time they spoke she told him the sweetest thing he ever heard from a female, and never forgot what she told him. He frequently thought of Jessy-Lynn, his wife, in his private thoughts, until he was fourteen years old, and eventually he forgot about her when he began fantasizing about his high school choir conductor. When Paula put her desires to him bluntly, in that moment, he imagined his wife who had lived across the street. He wondered if his favourite toy car was still buried in her sandbox for her to delightfully discover one day.

"Take me then," he said.

They held hands and she led him into her room. He lay down on her mat as she opened her dresser for a pill bottle. "What's that?" he asked. "It's Clonazepam," she said. She turned off the light and took off her underwear, slid off her bra and knelt down on the mat, atop Vic. At that moment there was a loud knocking at the front door. "Don't worry about that," she said. She felt his legs and stomach and Vic became very aroused. "You were making quite a bit of noise. Let me go check who that is," he said and went upstairs to the door.

Vic opened the door and it was two police officers. Vic was scared and felt intimidated.

"Are you Victor Glatt?" the officer on the step said.

"Yes."

"Do you know Paula Hansen?"

"Yes."

"Have you been making a lot of noise tonight?"

"No, I was asleep most of the night."

"Well, we have a report from Paula that you were making a lot of noise tonight. Can we come in?" Victor didn't say anything and turned around to turn on the light on the front step. As he reached for the light, the police officer came in the door, almost knocking Vic down.

"So, we don't hear any noise right now, but we just have to notify you to keep it down," the same police officer said.

"But I wasn't making any noise."

"I don't want to have to repeat myself. A Paula Hansen reported that you were making a lot of noise tonight, and we just want to make sure that you are not breaking the bylaw," he said. "Do you know Paula Hansen?" he asked again.

"Yes, I do. I was with her tonight."

"Well, she specifically told the dispatch that she wishes for you to stay away from her."

"What?"

"Am I not making myself clear?" The police had slowly crept into the landing as far as the steps to the main floor of the house, which pressed Vic back until he tripped over the stairs trying go up them, still facing the police officers, afraid of what they might do. The officer that had spoken reminded Vic of a bully he had in high school who once beat him with a skateboard, for money.

"I wasn't making any noise though," Vic repeated, finally reaching the top of the stairs.

"Do you know Paula Hansen?"

"Yes."

"She reported that you were making noise tonight."

"She's ..." Vic reeled his finger around his ear to signify that Paula was crazy.

"I think we're going to have to write that down," the other officer said, holding the door open.

"Just keep down the noise, do you understand?" the first officer asked one last time.

"Yes, I understand."

"Okay, thank you, and stay away from Paula please," the police officer said and they quickly left.

Vic went to the picture window in the living room and watched the police officers sitting in their cruiser for about ten minutes before they left. Victor was worried. He went back to his room after finally going to the toilet. He flipped over the Lou Reed album and played it. He couldn't fall asleep before the side was over because he was too anxious.

He needed someone to speak to and he could only think of one person, so he sent a text message to the woman who invited him to the diner when he gave her his second-last cigarette. "Hi Sarah, it's the guy you spoke with at the diner a couple months ago, remember me?" he wrote. It was almost five o'clock in the morning so he wasn't expecting a response right away. Thinking she would eventually respond, Vic felt a little relieved and tried to fall asleep once more. Paula was already asleep.

Chapter Six

Sarah replied to Vic's late-night message the next afternoon. "Sorry, I speak to a lot of men in the diner. I never gave any of them my number," she wrote. Vic sent her a message as soon as he got her reply. "I gave you a cigarette and you invited me for breakfast with you. It's Victor." She finally remembered. Men see her in the diner and talk to her; some invite her to Tahiti; some ask if they can introduce her to their mother; some talk about their ex-wives being less beautiful than her. She remembered Vic. He was cool-headed and engaged by her. "Oh ya! Vic!" she wrote, "Why didn't you text me sooner?"

They planned to meet the next morning for breakfast at the diner. Sarah told him she eats there every morning because the owner is a friend of her father, and on top of a ten percent student discount, Ed, the owner, gives her an additional fifteen percent family discount. She said she's been eating the same breakfast there for two years. Vic mentioned in his text messages that there had been a tense situation at home, which he wasn't sure could be resolved. He suggested that she seemed very wise for her age and, therefore, would understand.

When he went to the diner at seven-thirty the next morning, after they greeted one another, Sarah quickly made sure things were clear with Vic. "Just curious: How old do you think I am?" Vic guessed twenty-two. She laughed. "I'm twenty-eight man. Thanks though," she admitted. Vic explained that it was difficult to gauge a woman's age in their neighbourhood because it was a college neighbourhood and almost everyone looks like they're in their early twenties.

She had her coffee, bagel and a biscuit as always, and Vic wasn't sure what to have so he ordered the same as her. Most times, Vic was rather indecisive. "Put it on my bill," she said, "so what have you been doing with your life?" she asked. They paused for a moment, looking at each other, and then laughed. "Okay, no, seriously though … I met a girl," Vic said.

She laughed. "So, you met a girl. You know, every great story begins with: I met a girl," she said. Maybe she was right—love seems to give more meaning to every bit of routine life hands us. "It's not like I'm in love, but …" he said, failing to describe his naivety and that he seemed to have suddenly become appealing to Paula. "But what?" Sarah asked.

"I've never been in love before, and …" Vic hesitated again.

"So, you *are* in love?"

"It's just … I'm new to this whole thing and there's a girl that … I think … wants me … bad. But she's a little … psycho."

"Okay, first off: start talking in complete sentences or she's not gonna want you much longer, and second, why is she psycho? Does she message you all the time? Show up randomly? Get mad when you talk to women?"

He explained to her that it wasn't quite like what she was imagining the situation to be and he got to the speed of what happened with Paula. He told her about the door-slamming, psychotic yelling in the middle of the night, and the police showing up. He told Sarah how he got involved with her, how it developed into this, and their great night together at the lake. "I don't really have anyone I can talk to," he said, "I'm not really sure what to do."

Vic listened as she spoke. She told him that all of the details of his story were common for her, that men throw down all of their sanity in claims that they belong with her, and when it doesn't work out, for whatever reason, their loss of sanity being one of the reasons, they blame Sarah for driving them crazy. "And sometimes—rarely—but sometimes, this kind of thing happens to men," she said. It wasn't quite what he wanted to hear. "You don't want to make the wrong person itchy by scratching," she concluded.

"This is what I meant by, *they don't exist when they aren't around*. Put all of that girl's convoluted energy out of your mind right now, and any other time for that matter, because none of it exists. None of it. The only time it's real is when you're faced with it. In that moment, and only that moment, you have sympathy for it. If she feels there is some indivisible connection, know that it is only her convoluted energy driving her to that conclusion."

"Don't you think that's a little insensitive?" he said.

"Let me tell you a story," she said. "I was walking down-town yesterday and there's two guys standing in front of the Sally Anny, dirt as fuck, and a guy pulls up in a decked out corvette waiting for some old guy to cross the street. So, what do these dirt-fucks do? They go up to the guy's window and say: 'hey, we see you got a hundred-and-twenty-thousand dollar car there, you think you can spare five dollars."

"Ya, and?"

"Well, what if that guy's wife just left him and he's got no money for the alimony, or he just lost his job and he's living the last few dollars of his savings, or God knows what other possibility it might be. Maybe he's living paycheck to paycheck, leasing a car he can just barely afford."

"Okay, true."

"And the thing is: are they gonna understand that story? Are they gonna feel sympathy? They see him in that car and he's the picture of success—just like to that girl you are her love story. What's her name?"

"Paula."

"Right. Paula. Do you know what I mean?"

"No, not really."

"There *is* another option. Do you want to hear it?"

"Thank God, yes I do."

"You can have no love for her, and use her for your own sexual urges until even that fails to satisfy—actually it will start to cause you grief and displeasure, and eventually you will get to the point I'm making anyway. Eventually nothing changes."

"Okay, now I get what you're saying."

"See? I mean, eventually everything changes because this happens to women way too much, but in this case, eventually nothing changes."

"Right," Vic said and they paused their discussion and for a few seconds and then looked at each other and laughed.

After a few seconds of silence, Sarah asked: "So, you've

really never been with a woman? What exactly did you mean by that?"

"Well, there was a girl ... she was seven years old ..." Then Sarah interrupted.

"Are you some kind of ..." Vic stopped her immediately.

"I was the same age," Vic continued. "We got married when we were seven. Her brother was the priest. She moved away, and then I moved away and now I'm here, really far away from there. Before she left, she told me when she grew up, she would lock herself in her room until I came for her; she wanted no one else to have her."

"So, that's it then? You were married when you were seven and you waited for her until you were thirty-one, after she left you for over two decades?"

"I guess. I was a little lost. But I've got an idea."

"What's that?"

"I'm gonna lock myself up until *I find me.*"

"I've got a better idea. You go to the college right? I'm going back to school. I'll be there, you'll be there. Let's be best buds!"

"I do go to the college, and it sounds like a plan. Doesn't it start next week?"

"Yep."

"Paula's gonna be there."

"Not if you don't see her there."

"I guess," he said and they finished up their breakfast, Sarah paid the bill, they had a cigarette outside the diner and everything was dandy. They made plans to meet on Tuesday, the first day of classes. Sarah was going to the grocery store. Vic went home and listened to the entirety of the same Lou

Reed album, starting from the first side. After, he went out the back door to have a cigarette, trying to avoid seeing Paula on the front step.

Part Two

Chapter One

Sunday September 3, 2017

We suffer from heartbreak for our entire lives and then we get heart disease and die. It says it right on the package—leading cause of heart disease—*is it?* It still hurts to think of the deaths but the addiction is hard to kick. We hold onto cigarettes more than they hold onto us. The only benefit, as I see, is that, more so than generosity and kindness, smoking attracts people. It attracts the wrong kind of people—people that although they smoke cigarettes, are capable of changing the course of your life for better or for worse. Paula and Sarah were that, but I think writing about it, and the ego trip of writing a book caused me to have a downturn in my luck. Not to mention the book was about loving the wrong woman.

However, fifteen years as a smoker will put you in a lot of situations with people who were segregated from anyone who doesn't smoke, and sometimes pairings with the unwelcome people grow into superfluous bonds. What's the likelihood that any of those happenstance run-ins turn into a deeper bond?—but moreover, with the pariahs that stick around, not only to wade, what's the likelihood you won't suffer rejection, humiliation, suicidal thoughts, or just feel something so entirely superfluous that you get in over your head? Anything can go wrong, especially living in an house with a twenty year old Venezuelan, self-proclaimed spiritual advisor, who doesn't like smokers.

Meeting Mateo for the first time, he suggested quitting. If you smoke, you don't love yourself—that was his argument. But then again, maybe you shouldn't trust a person who: rejects any popular ideas that come from science; that suggests everything our society comes to realize is true is not true, that anything the media says is a hoax; that still requires a source for information, deeming that only the sources that perpetuate conspiracy theories are legitimate; and who cannot afford a bed and puts one he found on the side of the street in his bedroom in the house you share.

The cause of the bedbugs could have been: the abundance of used books, used vinyl records, or the used clothing; the cat or the mice; the African teenager that lived in the basement whose wafting body odour prevented me from going anywhere in the basement or near the door at the top of the steps; the large, old, stereo speakers I pilfered from the garage; the overnight visits to Carly's house; or maybe—just maybe—it was the overly-assertive, ideology-pushing, condescending, Venezuelan life advisor (spiritual advisor, or whatever you want to call it), who boasted that he could provide you with a *yoga-cum-meditation* degree.

Luckily, I live in Canada and although you hear a lot about heat treatments, you can store all of your belongings in an outdoor storage facility through the winter and that'll take care of the bedbugs. There aren't really any other benefits to winter.

Mateo and I moved from there, I had just graduated, had a new job, a new place, and within months I was backing out on the rent with no place to live, begging the landlord for my last month rent back and all my pay going towards an outdoor storage space for all of my stuff because all of my stuff was still contaminated.

On top of that, the bedbugs were causing a little bit of a Kafkaesque delusional episode which was likely expounded by the lasting effects of a past incident—a hallucinatory journey into literature, brought on by an attempt at self-deprivation—from heartbreak—self-deprivation to become whole. I'm sure it will come up if anything reminds me of it.

Moving on ... I haven't seen Sarah or Paula since April two years ago. I'd rather not think about what happened, or that their absences have left me quite lonely, and questioning the morality of my writing. I try to focus on selling my books, but even still, I went on a dating site to meet some women, make a connection, or get some action, but the women I met there seemed to be more interested in my book than they were in me. I've talked to three women on a dating site over the summer and all of them bought my book. They read it, then they stopped talking to me. I've decided that my new book marketing strategy is going to be sweet-talking women on dating sites.

Carly hasn't been around much either; not since the summer one year ago. Her quick and timely emergence into my life was quite a thing of synchronicity. I'll say that for sure. But I'll get to the affairs with Carly at some other point because from time to time she has a habit of swooning back into my life, or you could say, in and out of the lives of several different gentlemen.

But, there are also the sideliners, the ladies that, for whatever reason, have an ongoing stake of superficiality in my life. Like yesterday, I went to an end-of-summer festival down by the lake and talked to a woman I met at a book show a month ago. She had a vendor booth at the festival. We talked for a few minutes but ultimately it wasn't the right place for conversation to go beyond small talk, and in all of the times I've experienced with her—a compliment on my shirt at the book show; meeting her for coffee so she could give me an oversized teacup that could double as a soup bowl (as a means to free up some of her apartment space); an invitation to see a superhero movie sometime (which doesn't appeal to me since I haven't desired to see a movie in well over two years)—there has been no apparent reason to believe she ever communicates anything other than small talk.

So, I wander aimlessly, walking or riding the bus and reading, or riding my wheels with no place to go, and nothing to do. Although loneliness is a quality that we all must endure (sometimes even while we are with someone), in every instance of it that I can think of, there is always an intervening event that rips you up in the end, apprehensively targets the tedium at first and crescendoes into an aggressive stranglehold of the heart. And I'll willfully let that happen again, but it's unpredictable when it will occur.

I can't say that Mateo was totally bad, because as the time came when I was about to publish the book last year, he was very supportive. But at the same time, the increasing infestation made it difficult to sleep. I never did find a new place after the bed bugs took over. Mateo returned to Venezuela, denying his involvement in the bug problem, and I resolved to move back in with my parents, in the apartment where I had started my college studies before I moved to Etherington three years ago. I quit my job, and after biding my stay last winter, spring, and summer, with my parents, and a year out of college, I'm starting at the college again on Tuesday.

Chapter Two

Wednesday September 5, 2017

I had classes today, but there were no classes when I went to the college on Tuesday. There was free pizza yesterday, gift bags with non-lubricated condoms, body wash, and lube, lineups for student cards, new timetables, and contests to win free Mars bars. It was supposed to rain so I took the bus. I had to buy a book for my first class of the semester, so I waited in the lineup at the bookstore.

Near the end of the day, after it had rained a bit and the booths in the college courtyard closed, everyone had eaten too much free pizza to contend for more Mars bars. At that point, I ran into Samantha. She goes by Sam. She reminds me of Sarah, but not physically. Sam is wiry and Sarah had a bit more stature to her. "Hey! You're the unicycle guy aren't you? I see you everywhere. Do you have your unicycle today?" she said. I didn't ride my unicycle because of the call for rain. Nonetheless, Sam needed a cigarette, and I had some.

We sat on the steps outside one of the buildings of the college as she waited for her boyfriend, hardly talking, a bit hazed, lethargic, like the comedown after toking a spliff, sunlight beaming occasionally through the waning clouds. She has a very assertive, bubbly personality, but she doesn't talk a lot unless she has something to say to you. It's a treat because many people, when they know they're bubbly, they obnoxiously speak whenever they can think of something to verbalize, asserting their charisma as much as they can.

"I wish I had some money. I'd go into the bar for a beer," I said. So, Sam offered to buy me a beer, and we went in. She's twenty-one years old, has a kid, and her boyfriend is five years younger than me. She offered to buy me food too, but I told her I wasn't very hungry and that I would rather just have more beer. "So, what's the deal with the unicycle?" she asked.

I told her a bit about unicycles. "The unicycle is the ultimate symbol of autonomy—with the adversity of only having one wheel, there is a struggle to move forward. When you grow more comfortable with your knowledge of the mechanics of the bike and the lay of the land, you learn to manoeuvre gracefully on any terrain life can throw at you. It's the same as the test of gaining your own autonomy. I started riding it at the end of last spring, as a form of non-violent, non-threatening rebellion," I told her. "You're an interesting kind of guy," she said, "So you're a lone wolf then, eh? Do you have a girlfriend?"

I told her that I wasn't very lucky with women—"women seem to abscond from the road of love, aimlessly. Although, there was one woman—she was a bit of a lunatic, sweet for the most part, but she left too. I'm not that picky, but the overwhelming feeling I attract is disinterest, which itself is actually an admirable quality. In love, non-attachment is a falter because you can't really love someone that doesn't love you. The irony is that you have to attach to them so that they can love you. At the same time, though, attachment can be a falter. But in the big picture, the idea of opening your heart has to do with exposing your non-attachment in a way that it accepts another into unification.

"You speak really well," she said, "are you a writer or something?"

"I've written a book once."

"What's the book about?"

"Well, I locked myself in a room, wrote a book about heartbreak, and the day I got out, the women I loved had disappeared. I mean, they didn't really disappear, but they absconded—one is dead. I was in the hospital when she died. I got a little sick while I was locked up, hallucinating from not eating and from the bleach fumes, and when I got out of the hospital I edited it and published it. It's actually quite a poetic book."

"What the fuck? That sounds like a mind-fuck. I gotta read it," she said, excitedly.

"That's what all the girls say on the dating sites."

"Me and Giles are planning to go to the bookstore and pick out a book tomorrow. We're starting a book club for lovers. Wanna join?"

"Nah, it's okay. I'll let the two love-birds do that together."

"Okay. Your loss. So, what kind of music do you like? You look like a grunge type of guy. Don't tell me: you're into Nirvana."

She wasn't too far off. I was wearing black jeans, white Adidas sneakers, and a black Levi's jacket. I was missing only one thing from the getup—if I had a black Cadillac I would have been a veritable *Time Bomb*, á la the punk band Rancid. So, I showed her the playlist of songs I had on my phone. I had *Blackbird* and *Norwegian Wood* on the playlist. She commented that she wasn't really a Beatles fan.

"You need a great playlist to stay happy," I said. "If you aren't happy, you need to go and fix your playlist. Most people put sad music that reminds them of times of love on their playlist. That's wrong. I'm lucky: The Beatles should be tainted by heartbreak by now, but they aren't. The Beatles are un-taint-able. I read a book by Haruki Murakami about a guy hearing *Norwegian Wood* on a plane, and when he heard it, he was reminded of a tragic love story that had unfolded in his life. It's actually really a great book, other than the fact that I don't believe The Beatles' music can be tainted. Murakami is great, but he's full-o-shit in that respect. You and Giles should get that book."

"Well, I said I'm not a big Beatles fan, but maybe. What's his name?"

"Murakami," I said and spelled out the letters. "Riders on the Storm, though, that one kills me every time."

"What's your book called?"

"Riders on the Storm."

She laughed. "You're something else. I think you're one of those people you just have an instant connection with. We will be good friends. You like deep things. You aren't skin-deep," she said. And at the time, I was thinking our conversation was only skin-deep. "You probably don't have much luck with women because you know what you want and you don't put yourself in a position to lose yourself before you know it's right. Most people do it the other way around, you know?" she said.

The waitress came and Sam ordered another round of beers and a plate of sweet potato fries. The fries came and she picked at the fries, only eating a couple. She went to the bathroom shortly after and I started to eat some of the fries even though I said I didn't want any. By the time Sam came back from the bathroom there were hardly any left. "I'm sorry. I ate most of them and you hardly got any," I said. "Didn't you see me? I ate almost all of them," she said.

The inconsistency of my perception got to me. I thought I ate most of the fries, but she thought she did. She began sending text messages to her boyfriend as he was almost at the bar to join us. I debated in my mind the validity of my perception. Has my perception always been inaccurate? I'm telling you this story—I've been through intense hallucinatory states—I'm not even sure how valid my accounts are, especially at the point where the beer took over, and I was so uninhibited of everything, potentially including my ability to recount actuality.

Giles came. My perception at the time allowed me to believe that he liked me a lot. Sam kept buying the three of us rounds of beer. I told her that we should leave the bar and grab a few beers at the beer store and drink in the park, that it would be less expensive. So that's what we did. Her daughter and parents were away with family in Montreal for the week, so she had her house to herself. We waited for another rain shower to stop and then we set out for the beer store.

Giles went off to take Sam's dog for a walk while I went to

get beer with Sam. As Sam and I walked through the college parking lot, I noticed a couple of kids using a wooden pallet to climb onto the roof of one of the old, unused college buildings. "You know, you can get to the top of that building if you place one of the skids on the first roof. I wouldn't recommend going to the top of that building when you're drunk though. You could fall and die."

"Where are we? Where are we going?" Sam asked. She was clearly drunk. The sun was heating us quite nicely, shining through the rain clouds that had passed us.

"We're going to the beer store for beer," I explained to her. "Just follow me."

Sam was drunk, lost, and almost confusing me as to where we were, where we were heading, and then we found the beer store as a result of my perseverance to get more free beer at Sam's expense. Giles caught up with us with the dog. I can't remember the dog's name because I got quite drunk last night. The dog wasn't as much a dog, but rather a pony for a five-year-old child, and he might have bit my nuts off if he wasn't so docile. Sam bought twelve tall cans of beer at the beer store. First, we took the twelve tall cans of beer up into the apartment where I live with my parents. Sam, Giles and I drank beer and smoked cigarettes on the balcony.

After a while, I offered to make them some food, but Sam wanted pizza. She took us to the pizza place halfway between my parents' apartment and her house. She paid for a round of slices for the three of us. By the time we went out for pizza, I was smoking Sam and Giles' cigarettes because I ran out of my own. Then we went back to Sam's place and finished off the rest of the beers. As we got to the last couple of beers, Sam packed some pot into a vapourizer and we went out to the patio to toke.

I talked to Giles all night about writing. He has a deal with one of the big Canadian publishers for a trilogy. He just doesn't know how to start the second in the series. He says he's come a long way since writing the first one and to keep the writing style of the first one would be more of a headache than a blessing. He's torn as a writer—compelled by authenticity, but swayed by the ego trip of being accepted by others.

Maybe my perception isn't so precise when I'm drunk—maybe they didn't like me as much as I thought. After my first class today, the first of the year, and after sitting with the same girl in all of my classes for the day (the same girl who also followed me around all day in between classes) I realized, acutely, that I will not be seeing Sam and Giles very much anymore. I made an impression, a good lasting one, but I took too much from them. In case you didn't notice, I pushed Sam to provide for me more than any one good adult person should ask for. And in that sense, I've exhausted their future generosity and desire to accompany me. It was still a great first day back at the old college try.

Chapter Three

Sunday November 5, 2017

I met Adam in homeroom in the fall of 1997. That dingy homeroom had concrete floors, metal shingles on the walls and looked like the back of a dump truck. In those days, that particular high school was mostly boys, and only a few girls, since it had just recently changed its policy to accept girls. I say boys, but in grade nine, some of the older boys looked like full-grown men to me. Many of them looked and acted like criminals. I thought I was a bit of a class clown before high school, but some of these boys were not only class clowns, but ruthless, and acid-tongued, and I became wary of men at that time.

A few months into high school I became aware of Adam. For some reason, he glanced at me one day, and when he did, I felt something—I saw something—something came from his blue eyes into me. From then on, proximity brought us together. We had mutual friends, mutual interests and he stood out among the miscreants that us men didn't realize we had grown into by the end of high school. Adam Percy stuck by. That is to say: when proximity failed to bring us together, the proximity of our hearts kept astride in a far-reaching lilt of togetherness.

For most of our lives proximity is the single-most consolidating factor in relationships. My wife lived across the street, I lived in a house with Paula, and I knew Sarah only when I moved into her neighbourhood. It takes a certain kind of bond to extend a relationship beyond its defining quality of proximity into something far-reaching. The proximity of the heart and soul doesn't necessarily equate to the proximity of the body. Knowing this, what's out there in this great wide world for me, for you, for humanity? I have expressed that my first experience with Adam was ethereal—a feeling, as a young boy, I wasn't yet harmonized with, but would later become a defining factor in everything that has evolved me.

As I experience evermore connectivity to the spiritual world, in tune, and receptive, I feel as though I'm a vessel. A vessel of what, you might ask. Plainly speaking, I am a vessel of the omnipotent—a beneficent omnipotence that has me thinking that there are so many injustices in the world and that I am not here to live undirected and therefore haplessly sauntering though life, but to experience what the omnipotent has to show me so that I may tell it to the world, and improve the potential of others who may not be so perceptive of ethereal transcendence.

I told Adam that I felt I was a vessel in the past summer.

And you know what? He feels like he is too. Realistically speaking, he was an electrician. He lived in a home with his wife and children on the coast of the Pacific Ocean, and recently, according to something I am not fully aware of, yet, he has moved back to Ottawa (where he lived during his university years) to study theology with Dominican Monks. So, he's an electrician turned theologian. But, it doesn't shock me so much because he only became an electrician to provide for himself financially after studying Philosophy in university.

Now that Adam is closer to where I reside on Lake Simcoe, I feel I may be able to visit him again. I will make arrangements soon enough. But, until then, I had to get out, and something was calling me to Toronto—to Glenn Gould, who sits in Toronto, as a bronze statue on a bench in front of the CBC.

Glenn Gould died the same day I was born.

Upon hearing of the story of Glenn Gould, I felt an affinity with him. He spent most of his time in a cabin on Lake Simcoe, was a tremendous pianist, and later in life took obscene amounts of prescribed medications for illnesses, which may or may not have been correctly diagnosed, resultant of his brilliant, but tumultuous mind. And then he died thirty-five years ago, on October fourth, at fifty years old, about seven hours before my birth.

Like Gould, I go, every day, to a little diner in a Lake Simcoe city. Although he ate a completely different meal than me; his at supper, mine at breakfast; and I eat a bagel and a biscuit with a coffee, because that's what I used to eat every day with Sarah when we went there for breakfast everyday starting in the fall three years ago. Every morning before school we went to the diner together, she ordered her usual and I ordered a coffee, and then we went off to our respective classes. We spent every moment together in between classes as well. Looking back on it, it's difficult for me to think of a time when I wasn't with Sarah, until I withdrew myself from life, from her, and from what I'm now assuming was a kind of powerful love that tried to transcend the aloofness of my perceptivity at the time.

So, as we spent every bit of time together, Paula was at the college that year. Paula lived in the same house as me, and there was an incident between us while I spent all of my time with Sarah. Paula, I would say, didn't really love me the way Sarah did. Sarah's love was consistent and full-figured, with arms and legs, feet, toes, and fingertips, but the feelings of Paula were like a mannequin in a window, that was undressed by others, and took you for someone like her—but I *was* like her—at the time.

Paula watched Sarah and I together at the college. I would see Paula there, and when I did, she existed. When I didn't see her, she did not exist. I thought this way because this is how Sarah told me to think of Paula. She stared at us sometimes and when I caught her staring she would quickly look away as if she was looking, with ennui, right through us into the distance. She had something in mind, which I will get to on another day. Around that time there was a man that visited Paula almost daily with a big malamute.

At the time, the fall of 2014, I had just completed reading the book *The Girl with the Dragon Tattoo*. I read it on the couch in front of the big picture window. That room, in the house we lived in, was right above Paula's bedroom, and as I read on December first, in 2014, I heard the sounds of Paula's lovemaking coming up into the living room through the vents. I went over to the vent and lay down, putting my ear to the vent to listen more closely. As much as Paula was once the person that made me feel the greatest I had ever felt, up to that moment, I felt as horribly as I ever did when I heard the sounds of her lovemaking. It was the most horrible I've ever felt until I found out about Sarah.

So, Sarah and I had our breakfasts together, I smoked cigarettes with her (although she was trying to quit and only smoked sparingly) between classes, and I would occasionally collect bags of popcorn, toilet paper and bottles of bleach. When I heard Paula making love to the man with the dog, I put my collection of these things into action. I went to the Ministry of Community and Social Services to make sure that my disability cheque that came at the end of every month would be deposited directly into my bank account rather than sent by mail. Then I came home and emptied the bottles into smaller jugs, cut off the tops of my large distilled water bottles with a hacksaw, poured some bleach into the large water bottles and left all of the bottles in my closet, in large boxes. Then I took my door knob off of the door and put it back on so the lock was on the outside of the door. I had twenty bags of popcorn in my room. I had given my landlord post-dated cheques, put my telephone into the garbage can, and all that remained to do was lock the door knob, grab a knife to jimmy the door shut, locking myself up from the world, leaving it open to anyone who wanted to see me, including my separated self.

Soon after I withdrew from everything, Sarah started coming to see me on Fridays. Each time she brought with her a bottle of whiskey and we drank it in my room. I told her she could come but I wouldn't be able to let her in, and that she would always have to lock the door from the outside when she left. She started visiting me in the middle of December. I was still shaken by Paula, writing my book about the heartbreak I experienced as a result of her being with that man with the dog.

I rationed my popcorn, but by February I was almost out of food, and I noticed I had started to lose a significant amount of weight and was beginning to have hallucinations. I'm not quite sure if, at some point, Sarah sneaked in while I was in the middle of a hallucination, or if I left my room, but I began seeing my breath in the air quite frequently and empty bottles of Jack Daniel's would appear in my room occasionally. Because of the insistent hallucinations, I'm not quite certain how many times a week Sarah actually visited after February. I would occasionally blow the air into an O and I became aware that I was in control of my hallucinations. I *was completely* in control of them; I could have easily followed Sarah out into the cold winter nights to the donut shop on the corner to get what I needed, but I was too hard-headed to see reality.

If I saw reality—before I published my book, before I mistook Paula's action for meaningful, before I took my life for some kind of joke, I would have been able to live life in a vacuum. I would be able to go through life ignorant of any meaning, happy as a child in a sandbox, ignorant of death and love—but no—that all matters to me now. And the only reason it matters to me is the irony that before Sarah left, I realized life like an ignoramus so much so that it finally pushed me into seeing reality. Sadly, what happened to Sarah and I is something that reality magnifies like a painful past—and only perception of the beneficent and maleficent omnipotence allows a person to work on themselves to get better.

I'll get to it all. I'll tell you the whole story, bit by excruciating bit, but it's difficult to release it all, with all of the tears in my eyes, and all of the hurt that I am unable to requite, other than by living freely, perceptively, and aware.

But in my recent awareness, like I said, I visited Glenn Gould in Toronto, because I feel an affinity with him. I just turned thirty-five, got a new job as a barista, made a friend at work (by proximity of course), and took off with him and my first paycheck on a coach to Glenn's bench at the CBC.

Chapter Four

Wednesday November 15· 2017

The problem with pubs is you really only need one pint, and then you start to get the feeling you aren't alone there; that drinking is not such a bad thing; that surely all the people drinking in the pub are decent, and then you stay for three, four pints, and soon enough you're spending your last dime there. A good pub can make a man go completely broke, but totally remove him from his actual loneliness. I spoke on the phone with Adam while I was in the pub last night. He was reading Ezra Pound and I was biding my time until the bus came. But the bus came, and then another came, and then I had had three pints before I caught the last bus.

Before I went to the pub, I was at the college campus downtown working on some art designs well into the early darkness of the November nights. Sadly, because of my outing to the pub, I don't have much money left until payday tomorrow, and I'm plagued with the memory of November becoming December. There's something about November passing on into December, at midnight, cold and bleak. Something magical happens. I'm keen to describe it as an event that is similar, but opposite, to that moment when you're with a woman, and she flicks off the light, and you know you're going into the gourd—your heart opens up like opening the cupboard where you keep the tea and sugar, that sugary smell hits you, and suddenly life is every sweet little thing you imagined it would be—yes, the stroke of December, at midnight, is the opposite of that. With one flick of a season's wrist, darkness and decay seep through anything and everything and open a rotten gourd, at which one could curse.

There are a couple of things that wash away the rotten gourd of December: love, music, the stars on a clear night, the lake, art, and writing—but nothing compares to love. I'm sure when you're a kid, something like the Santa Clause parade does the trick, but when you're thirty-five, nothing really compares to a woman who cares for you, and the feeling that she could love you. Nothing really compares to any of that because you aren't expecting any of it, you've come to expect disinterest and ennui, but a few times you get a ripe one at the end of November, and suddenly the taiga isn't so bad.

I remember it like it was yesterday, and yesterday couldn't be farther away but so close to my heart, the first time Sarah came over in the middle of November in 2014. We had a connection with our music tastes, particularly with the music of The Beatles, and watched music videos on my television in my room, drinking the best cheap wine you can get at the Liquor Control Board of Ontario. And somewhere in the background (although that background was oblique as the midnight sky at the stroke of December because I was in the foreground for the first time in my life) the song, *This Must Be the Place*, by Talking Heads played. I told her, or anyone, for the first time, that I had schizophrenia.

She told me that she would never have suspected it. As I see it, the stigma that we have associated in our minds, with schizophrenia, doesn't quite align with what the disease actually is, or means. And then she flicked off the light and came to sit on my lap. There was a dull, flickering light from the music video on the television screen. She told me that she would be my therapist from then on and that she would come over to hear what my mind was distilling. She actually used the word distill, which threw me aback. Then, with her big bottom on my crossed legs, her heaviness only the weight of a grain of salt (with which I should probably take this moment in my life) that I could hold there for hours if she wished, I felt the urge to press my lips against hers. I would say that I felt like kissing her, but I had never kissed a woman before and I felt my attempt would be something akin to a primitive man polishing an antique armoire with a smooth rock.

She didn't seem to be turned off by me, but as it became clear that I was looking to kiss her, she got off of my lap. I felt a sensation that she was nervous to be so sensual with me; that she wasn't sure if she'd be indulging in her amorous senses, or being truly loving. The song had stopped playing and it was time to change the song. "It suddenly got really quiet in here," she said. She went over to the computer and played a song by The Smiths, although I shudder to think that this particular song had any meaning aligned with the closeness of us in that moment, but *How Soon is Now?* by The Smiths seemed to be apropos.

"More wine?" she said. I handed over my glass and she poured some for me. "Why don't we make sex noises so your roommates think we're getting it on? You know that's what they think we're doing, right?" I adamantly refused to go along with her idea, and I assume that she was joking, however, in becoming so moxie it was evident that she had attempted to cross the relationship into a new level—she had made it evident—I displayed only reticence in forestalling to kiss her.

Our relationship continued, and if anything, she appreciated me more than any other man because I was unique in that I had schizophrenia. She never once held it against me, or regarded me in ill light. I have always, always expected the opposite, and in seeing her openness and acceptance to me, it removed, partially or wholly, one of the filters that obfuscated a part of my view on the world; the belief that I will or won't be loved. Love can be just a *raison d'etre* amid the Borealis of the commonplace life but it also transcends and ascends the heart—the inclined heart as well as the declined heart—and soul, anywhere, anytime, any season.

In the dark places I live and stay, I am ever-wary of selflessness. I am wary of altruism. I question the validity of selflessness and altruism. That is not to say that neither exist within me, but rather that neither are commonplace motives for people. I fear that much of the world has come to accept this, my self-reflective aphorism as their self-reflection too, and thus it makes love, sadly, not very catchy, not very marketable. It makes love not true, but rather an ego trip. To the people like me, we see love as a dubious gesture in its rarity, making it all-too-difficult to accept.

In actuality, I felt that Sarah loved me, which altogether isn't a bad thing. But in the *vista grande*, the person accepting intimate love is usually not being altruistic. It would have been much better if Sarah loved everyone, everything, and herself, but that wasn't the case.

I long for her love for me once again but I know that it is only self-serving to wish for it, that actually true love is a love for everything, unwaveringly. Love can prevent war; love can prevent lies; love can prevent sadness. I long to feel a love such as this, and I'm not sure I would ever wish self-loathing to permeate someone's essence because a self-serving love was unrequited, but that result seems to be the powers that be.

I am talking about intelligent people—good natured, good hearted, intelligent people—that will realize immediately that you have not been conquered by love, but rather been conquered by your ego, and even still, for a while in the permanence of the Decembers of life, a love like Sarah's has a great deal of meaning. Authenticity aside, I would have gladly accepted her, her love, and been happy with it in my saturated ego. I'm pretty sure I wrote my book as a means to prolong the ego boost I received from the inclination that Paula loved me in her ostensibly loving progressions, but I took sex for love in those days, and Sarah eventually and mercilessly showed me the truth.

Sarah was quite ebullient. She accentuated my darkness. When you are brooding, people say you're too brooding and when you are lively, people say you're too lively. You can never win. Together the two of us made an excellent pairing. I accepted her for being so vivacious, and she accepted me in my depths and together there was a balance. Really, inside of every gloomy man resides a part of him that wants to be vibrant, and I saw the opposite in Sarah. She always wanted to be more deep, deliberate, and introspective. If she was hiding that part of her, she hid it well because I never saw it.

Before she sat on my lap in my bedroom that night, we took the first bottle of white wine of the night to the college parking lot where there were unused storage buildings and unused signs and shipping pallets scattered around. We took one of the pallets and propped it up against the side of one of the buildings, on the landing to the door, and then I climbed onto the first roof. Then Sarah lifted one of the pallets to me to prop up on the lower roof so we could climb onto the high, second level of the building. Sarah pulled herself up and we both made our way to the top of the building. We drank wine and listened to music played through our tinny phone speakers, up there.

Looking down from the edge of the building, you could easily see that there were enough concrete blocks, wooden pallets with nails sticking out, and metal signs to kill you if you accidentally slid down the sloping roof. The danger of the situation made that particular time together not just a hang out, but an adventure. If she wasn't there I never would have went up there, but because she had something of an adventurous side, she thought nothing of the danger that surrounded us in that moment. In truth, I was probably a lot more scared than her. In truth, I was even scared of her, in that she seemed to have a boundless attitude toward everything.

Chapter Five

Thursday November 30, 2017

Sunday November 30, 2014 wasn't like today. Today it is very cold and there's snow on the ground. Three years ago, on this date, was one of the last times I saw Paula. The weather that day was a few degrees above ten degrees Celsius and there was only frost on the ground until mid-morning. I had gone for breakfast with Sarah in the morning, received my disability cheque (as did Paula), and went out for a walk to celebrate the fine weather of the day. It had been a hot year, and the end of November was no different.

When I got back from my walk Paula was sitting on the step at the front door and she grabbed my attention. "Vic, I need to talk to you," she said. I asked her what the matter was. I thought it was going to be a story about how I had become distant since her psychotic outburst in the summer. There was a side to her I wasn't quite sure I ever really wanted to see, once or again. But she didn't tell me about how I had distanced myself, or the ups and downs regarding the man who came by almost every day with some husky dog. "Sure, what is it?" I responded, as politely as I could.

"My mother had a heart attack," she told me, "I'm going back to Winnipeg to see her." She then asked me if she could borrow my phone so she could look up the bus schedule. There was some story about why she didn't have a phone anymore. I don't quite remember the details, but it was probably something to do with a poor person ostensibly befriending her and asking to borrow it on a promise, then subsequently realizing they had no intentions of giving the phone back—or being Paula's friend. Sadly, Paula was unable to mark people as either trustworthy or untrustworthy in most cases. For one, the guy with the husky looked like he had spent a few years doing time for something very bad, but I can't prove it, or maybe shouldn't even comment at all, but that's the feeling I had.

And then I looked up the number for her because she struggled to use the phone properly. You could tell she was in shock. I think my presence actually wasn't all that comforting to her, since she probably had become a little wary of me when I dropped out of her life. Then I told her the bus schedules and tried to explain where she had to go to pick up the bus tickets, but she was apprehensive to go on her own, so I told her I would take her there. "You drive?" she said. I could tell she didn't feel like walking and she probably wasn't even appreciative that the temperature was more than ten degrees above normal for the last day in November. For the most part, Paula was nice, but almost every time she spoke I was irked by her. Her presence on the other hand was very calming to me—I'm not sure if it was her aura or what. She seemingly didn't really have any sort of bad intentions for anyone in that uniquely maternal way.

I tried to make her feel comfortable when we walked to the station. I'm not quite sure what my intentions were but I took her on the same route as we took when we went to the lake in the summer that had just passed. She noticed it immediately.

"This looks familiar to me," she said. "Oh yeah?" I said, pretending like I wasn't leading her to that same spot. It was the middle of the afternoon but it gets dark around five o'clock at the end of November and even during the day there's mark-edly less people on the streets than in the summer.

I asked her about Winnipeg and if she was close to her mother. She told me a story of how she worked in a library and her co-workers used to tease her. "They were all so snooty," she said, "I had a breakdown on the bus home and when I got back to Winnipeg my mother was the only person that was there for me." She also told me that on the bus back to Win-nipeg, the words of one of her co-workers burned a hole in her mind. Her co-worker said to her, "Don't judge a book by its cover," but as Paula rode the bus back to her hometown in a delusional state (which she described as being *freaked out*), she repetitively thought of the phrase, in anguish, "Don't judge a book; buy its cover." Paula then told me that when she went home to Winnipeg she ripped out the pages of all of the books in her book collection and kept only the covers. Apparently Paula still has a kick-ass collection of book covers covering the entire wall of her old room.

I'm not quite sure what to think of that. Since the time she called the cops on me in a mad rage she always struck me as a loony, even in the look in her eyes. Still, I'm not sure what my intentions were, but the weather was nice. In the summer, people run up and down the staircase leading to the lake, exercising. In the middle of November there's truly no one to be found. "It's so peaceful here," she said as we arrived at the park overlooking the lake. "I think you said something like that the first time we came here," I told her. And then as if she had a jerking pain in her gut, she quickly bent forward like she was going to touch her toes and she paused with her stomach resting on her thigh and jerked herself back up. It was the most animated thing I have ever seen her do.

"I do remember this place," she said, looking at me straight in the eyes. I saw a little glint, the tiniest snicker, of incandescence in her eyes. "What was that song you sang me here?" she asked. We had paused and it was unspoken that we were admiring the view of the lake. We stood there admiring like a *fractal of nostalgia*. And I tried to sing *Dear Prudence* but she stopped me and told me that wasn't the song she had in mind. So I sang *Riders on the Storm*. I didn't really know the words to that song but I hit the hook. "That's my favourite song Vic, but that's not it. What was the other one?"

I had only sung two other songs that night we danced at the lake. It felt a little like she was narrowing us towards a conversation about somewhere that she wanted to go with me, to pounce, and I was hoping to go there with her.

I was embarrassed to sing the song I thought she was thinking of, so I started yelling, "Cre-e-am ..." and before I could say tangerine, she said, "no, no, the other one silly." And then it hit me! This is my first time with a woman! In a completely monotone voice, "Why don't we do it in the road?" I asked.

"Okay," she said a little too chipper, like she was seventeen and had just been asked go on a ride at an amusement park. She held out her hand. I'm not quite sure what happened to make her want the scene that had been cut out of the original version—the too-hot-for-television scene that everybody heard about but was still waiting to be leaked onto TMZ, but I did it! That was it! … Sorta.

I started kissing her furiously and groping at her body, trying to find all the treasures like they were really difficult to locate. And I gently nudged her to the ground to feel more relaxed than bending down or kneeling to kiss her. I kept kissing her furiously but I think possibly something was wrong because she didn't really return the intensity of my kisses. I undid my belt and I was already ready for her and she saw it. She pushed me down onto my back and straddled me.

She didn't really moan or scream or anything. She writhed on me mostly, deep inside her. Then she stopped. I could tell she was tired, so I put my knees up and gave it to her from underneath. She looked like she was concentrating on something painful to think of when I sparingly looked at her her face and then her delta. Her dress draped over our mid-sections but, curiously, I held up her dress to reveal it. And then after a few minutes she sighed in a way that, to think of it now, kind of reminds me of the sound from the release of a whale's blowhole. At the time, I was sort of thinking, *that's it?*

I tried for a little longer. I also tried to get on top of her but she wouldn't let me so I kept giving it to her from underneath until I almost tired myself. "Are you going to come for me?" she said. And I'm not sure if it was the Paliperidone injections I get every month or the cold, wet grass on my rear, but

I didn't. I resolved to say, "Yeah, I'm done," and I stopped. "Is this actually the way to the terminal," she asked as we were getting up. "The scenic route," I said, "the most scenic route I've been on all year," I embellished.

As I say, I'm not quite sure what my intentions were. I know now that it's best that I didn't go to her without protection, but I got caught up in a moment that maybe shouldn't really have happened in the first place. I can't take it back, and if I had known what would happen later, I definitely wouldn't have done it. I didn't really love her. I'm not even sure I cared about her.

Now, if you asked me what happened on the rest of the trip to the ticket booth at the bus terminal, it would be like asking a murderer to recall the events of his murder in an interrogation. If there's any one identifying characteristic of having sex, it's the state of euphoria afterwards that feels so good, so contiguous to the heavens like no other pleasure feels. I think that defining euphoria would have lasted me quite a long time, weeks, months, but the next day, at our old place on Etherington, I suffered a blow to the temple by Paula like no other I've ever felt, until things got intense with Sarah.

I mentioned this in an earlier entry, but I was finishing up *The Girl with the Dragon Tattoo* the next day, when I started to hear the impassioned sounds of Paula from the floor above her room—noises more impassioned than I had induced the day before. That December first, 2014, I started writing it all down. I, roadrunner, was struck by the heartbreak of Wile E. Coyote's anvil. As much as I thought I was impervious to heartbreak, stately as I was, for most of the day after my first sexual encounter, I was roadkill in the triggering moments of

Paula's duplicity—moments I would recall as outliers from the humdrum, in the book of ruminations on heartbreak that I wrote in my seclusion. In her defense, I suppose I was quite on the brink of ruin before that day.

Chapter Six

Monday December 18, 2017

I walked to the lookout this morning on my way to Ed's Diner. It takes me longer to get there, now that it's too cold to ride my unicycle. I've been walking there, on that route through the lookout, every morning in November and December to get breakfast. In a way I'm spiritually hailing Sarah to return by going there, but at the same time, it's a bit of self-deprecation towards the sentiment of my book—a book that attempts to hail Paula. Over the weekend, I got a few copies of my book to be displayed for sale on consignment at an art gallery overlooking the lake in the center of the city. When I arrived at work today, one of my co-workers asked me to sign a copy he just picked up at the art gallery over the weekend. And in the same sentiment as the women who bought it when they met me on dating sites, I have the slight feeling that the content of my book is going to get me fired from my new job, as soon as my co-worker reads it.

I read the first poem of it when I got back from work this morning, to somehow justify the book and all it represents, but I ceased up on the first stanza, knowing that it represents something other than me. I can look back on my time locked in my room, writing, as leading me to leave my room completely free—more fruitfully free than I ever had been—but also it shows that the intention to sell the book is an ultimatum of my ego—writing it was a genuine act, but to sell it is duplicitous because I abhor its content. You could imagine the schema I'm describing would be hard to mull over repetitively by reading it. Nonetheless, the opening lines read:

Phantasmagoria

I will comfort you at the nexus of the nightmare,
The ledge of the tipping point where you stand,
As you hold the newborn child, longing for your arms,
Away from the fearful reality of the dream,
Far from the frightening dreamscape of reality.

That's about as far as I got with it after work.

An old man at the diner talks to me on the streets when he sees me now. Randy is his name. "Hey there, young fella," he says, and I say hi back to him. I didn't know him at the time, but when I first started going to Ed's I once sat in Randy's usual spot. He wasn't upset. Now I know he chooses to sit in that spot because he can fit his walker on the other side of the table, and he was probably happy I sat there because it gave him a reason to talk to someone. He lives at the old folks' home down the street and I see him on the buses once in a while.

There's a group of men that sit at the large round table in the center of the restaurant. They talk about the news and the group of them never seem to come to a lull in conversation even though most of their conversations are exceedingly mundane. They aren't as old as Randy, but they're all retired.

I guess Randy would sit with them if there was space for his walker at the table. He's got a bad back, and it amazes me that he can walk the three or four blocks to the corner to get his scratch and win lotto tickets before going to the diner. I remember last year, just before spring, he still came every day when the sidewalks were completely glazed with ice.

I only stay there for a few minutes really. I'm just in and out, but I'm a regular there and the people that go to Ed's are the lonely sort. There are a lot fewer women than men at the diner, but the women there seem lonely as well. The only people that aren't lonely at the diner are Ed and his wife. They don't talk much though. Ed's wife looks like she probably has a daughter that's very close to her, and probably a little grandchild. The diner's been on that corner for as long as the oldest person in town would remember, yet Ed and his wife look like they're about seventy years old, and Ed still is always walking around talking to the people at the plaza, smoking his cigarettes. He's not much of a charmer, just an iconic figure in the community.

It's hard to put your finger on the specific reason why Sarah went there. It doesn't really seem like her kind of place. She exuded excitement from every angle, but even though I don't see her there anymore, there is a certain indistinguishable charm about the place. It's kind of like a dog that rolls onto his back in front of you and just begs to be rubbed. I don't know—they serve good biscuits, and if I stayed there long enough, I'd get free refills on coffee. But, I have my coffee to go, and then walk back to the lookout. When I reclaimed my freedom, I realized that we are afforded existence among beautiful things which don't make any effort to attract us other than existing; like the lake from the vantage point of the lookout. That's why I go to the lake; it's freedom. The view asks for nothing, I ask for nothing, yet all are pleased.

Now that I think of it, Ed gave me my breakfast on the house today. He said he was giving all the regulars their meals for free. "Anything you want today, on the house," he said, "an early Christmas present for the regulars." But, I told him I just wanted a bagel and a biscuit with a coffee to go. He tried to convince me to get the whole shebang. "Nah, just the usual," I told him. "Alrighty, coming up," he said. Then his wife started preparing it for me.

It's strange that he gave me a gift today, but today was the first day Sarah came over to see me in my seclusion three years ago. At first we talked about where I had been. I didn't show up to the diner to meet Sarah for a few weeks, and I didn't have my phone to respond to her (I'm lucky she even came or remembered where I lived. We were pretty drunk and it was dark the first time she came over). I never fully explained what it was I was doing with the door locked from outside and all the jumbo bags of popcorn. I'm not really sure I know either.

She looked at my records, and she saw an album she liked. "This is *you*. This is totally Vic," she said. "Don't look," she said, "I wanna surprise you." She pulled the album off of the shelf when I looked away. Then the first song of the album played. It was *Magical Mystery Tour,* by The Beatles. "You: You're a mystery tour. Roll up," she said and jumped onto my bed with me. "I love this album," I said. I still remember she got out of bed to flip over the album and started to dance as *Hello Goodbye* played on Side B. I'm not sure but I think she may have been a little drunk that night. We discussed watching the movie *Across the Universe.* She explained to me that it was a new musical that had all of The Beatles' music.

She didn't come back for what seemed like a couple of weeks. The next time she came over was a Friday, and she had had a few drinks from the bottle of Jack Daniel's she sidled in with. "Am I intruding?" she said with a cordial smile on her face and a glint from the bottle in her eye. "Hello! No, not at all. You can come anytime. I won't be able to let you in, but come anytime," I said, excited to see her.

"Have you ever wished that if you just stayed in bed all day you'd get jacked? Well, now you will," she said.

She came every Friday after that. I'm going to do my best to read through *Rider's on the Storm* (That's the name of my book) to put it into context over the next few weeks so I can figure out when it was that we watched *Across the Universe* and hopefully partake in a superfluous song and dance of libationary Christmas pining. I haven't watched television or a movie in almost two years (poetry and fiction is more my speed), but now is the time. Now is the time.

Chapter Seven

Thursday January 11, 2018

They weren't your typical bags of popcorn. The owners of the convenience store where I continually bought them, throughout the fall, must have made them at home and brought them in. They were about the size of small garbage bags with a label that said *Jumbo Popping Corn Treats* on them. I've never seen them anywhere else. They also had coloured popcorn, but that seemed a little too decadent for long-term rations. In my room, when I was incarcerated, I had stacks of those jumbo bags of popcorn.

Sarah came over with a bottle of Jack Daniel's as usual, and we watched *Across the Universe*. It's a good thing we didn't watch it in February because that's when I started hallucinating. Everything was swell that night with Sarah. I would be able to recall it fondly, but I'm a little hung over since I got a little too drunk watching it last night in my new place.

That's right. I moved out of my parent's place at the beginning of January and my first order of business was to get a handsome batch of beer and a bag of *Jumbo Popping Corn Treats*.

I had been gathering a small savings since I started working at the coffee shop in the fall, and due to the college teachers strike this year, my first semester will be complete tomorrow. Things seem to be falling into place for me nicely—hard to say what's to come. I mean, I was able to read most of my book of poems.

I discovered that it was early January that I watched *Across the Universe* with Sarah because in February I began writing about my Hallucinations, self-deprecating myself at the same time, but the last poem I remember writing, before things got a little wobbly in my head, was the poem about Freud's interpretations of dreams. The concept was that Freud believed that dreams were the true depiction of the self, and if I could ever be hypnotised that that state would be my true self. Under hypnosis, someone would finally be able to know the real me, despite not wanting that privilege myself. I told all of that in a poem.

As I remember it, we had a few drinks before Sarah took the DVD out of her purse to tout its cinematic wonders. I actually had a DVD player in my room that I never used. She put on the movie almost without asking me, insisting that it was the best movie ever. That moment solidified our union in the love of The Beatles. "Hey, I've got a crazy idea," she said. "Why don't we have some popcorn?" We laughed good and hearty at that one. I'm not sure she ever figured out what was going on with me in that room during those months. The whole venture was a little duplicitous on my part for not telling her the truth. Maybe she did figure it out. To be honest though, I didn't really want to eat my popcorn with her because I was trying to ration it for as long as I could.

Nonetheless, I loved the movie then and I loved the movie last night. It was much better with Sarah since we lay close together that night, but it wasn't much different in that I was hailing her memory last night.

We got a little drunk and she danced to some of the songs. "Don't you love it?" she kept repeating to me. "Don't you love it?" I suppose my emotions don't show completely clearly, but I did. After it was over, I told her that I probably wouldn't have liked it as much if I watched it without her. I could tell she was hurt by that—it was one of her favourites—but that comment was true whether I loved it immensely or hated it, watching it with her.

Last night, for the most part, I came away with the over-whelming feeling that I've lived most of my life for that moment and the related moments of that winter with Sarah.

To explain, I remember being obsessed with baseball and hockey as a young boy. We played street hockey every day after school, and in the summers, we played baseball without enough players to fill the bases. Still, amid those early inspirations, one day after school, I immediately went to the record player, when I arrived home, and put on a Beatles album. It was the first time I ever put on a record by myself. It was 1993 and I was ten years old. Nobody knew. I listened to it alone. There was something magical about that moment in my development as an adolescent. I struggle to put a term to the psychological occurrence, but the first experience with

The Beatles and that moment sharing their music with Sarah were trysts from normalcy.

The feeling that both of us felt comfortable together made it so that it wasn't quite a tryst, in the next meetings in my room. It became understood that we were part-and-parcel—delivered together—to be handled with care. And in our comfort of togetherness, we rediscovered a new tedium. To put this in a more positive light, we crossed a boundary together, and put up a new boundary that we both shared. But things got rather complex, especially for an inexperienced man (the newborn child as I described myself in my first poem).

But, something about those childhood moments with The Beatles allows those feelings to supersede the similar feelings I shared with Sarah. Something about the moments of a ten-year-old boy are more tender than even the first moments of the first love of a thirty-two-year-old. A thirty-two year old, I would assume, has grown calloused to a broad gamut of new experiences. I'm not saying that my experiences with Sarah were unappreciated in the slightest. I mean, every once in a while, you hear adults tell you about how learning the guitar changed their lives at a late age—or church—or Carl Jung—or Feng Shui—or knitting ... you get the picture.

As certain as it is that we are calloused by our twenties and thirties, it is as certain that something will soften the callous. Just as likely, we will not be moved as much as the things that moved us as children, but we will grow beyond what our static physical stature allows. It is certain, but not always timely. The moments after your body begins to stop growing are the moments when you are able to grow limitlessly beyond your body. At thirty-two, I was only just discovering this. It is the beneficent omnipotence allowing our ascension.

But in most of my recent days, as much as I feel as though I am the vessel of a beneficent omnipotence, internally I feel a maleficent omnipotence trying to mutiny on my insides.

Sometimes my thoughts are debasing, and I'm unable to repeat them because I'm not fully thinking them, but rather susceptible to them by force of maleficent omnipotence. The two forces are a paradox for me, but it is such that causes my illness, and is distilling to know that the beneficence is external, and, without specific effort, greater than one can control. Realizing the maleficence and that it can be accepted or denied, is the first step to enlightenment.

If we choose to see the external (the omnipotent beneficence) in its innate light, it wipes away the maleficence in our minds. Rest assured that the beneficence has been there for us begotten primordially.

In many ways, the moment with Sarah that I am currently ruminating is more important than what happened next, because it allows me to see toward the absolute best that life offers. However, I think about what happened next more frequently and with greater fervour.

Chapter Eight

Thursday February 8, 2018

The diner is closer now, but the lookout is farther away. It's been difficult to get out to the lookout every day since the weather has been below ten degrees Celsius. I'm still going to the diner every day for a bagel, biscuit, and coffee. There was one man that lived at my parents' apartment, who sits at the round table with all of the other retired men. He actually lived on the same floor as my parents. He saw me with all of my stuff on the day I moved. He was happy for me that I was moving out, and asked if he could move into my housing complex. I don't blame him—it's quite nice here. I told him that there was bi-weekly housekeeping, that the building itself was only two years old, and there is a gym.

I haven't been to the gym yet, but I'm going to have to soon because my time spent walking has shortened to only times of necessity. That is, I'll start walking regularly when the temperatures rise a little. It reminds me of one of the poems in my book. My buddy from work, who read my book, also liked that poem as well. It's quite coincidental that that particular poem came up when my friend discussed my book with me, after he finally finished it. He said the book was "lo-fi"— whatever that means. But he said the one poem in question stood out because it seemed older, like it had been written by a famous classic poet. The poem he mentioned was coincidental because it was telling of when I wanted to end my seclusion.

It reads:

Winter is the Message

Love was written in a message—
wound like a yarn, but was a note
in a secret fold of icy preserve.
(Does a frozen heart not easily shatter?)

And to unwind, if she so chose—
she'd find a blizzard of words that is its media,
that only April could foolishly unravel
like the last flurry of a winter blunder,

Should this note not thaw in April,
for love to mend?

Sarah came over the week before Valentine's Day in the winter of 2015. I had just finished writing that poem. I asked her what the date was. She told me it was the week before Valentine's Day. "When are you going to come out of here, Vic?" she asked me. "I've decided I'm going to stay in here until I run out of food or until April, whichever comes first. I've just decided that, this afternoon," I told her. "Well, don't you get bored in here? What do you do with your time?" she asked.

When she asked me this, I had already completed three-quarters of my manuscript, reworked and edited all of it almost to completion, and was rather proud of the accomplishment. "Hold on one minute," I told her. I went over to my laptop and pulled up the last poem I wrote, *Winter is the Message,* and I printed it off for her. I had a box of envelopes in my closet. I opened my closet to get an envelope and the smell from the latrines hit me, so I quickly grabbed one, knocking more of them onto the floor of the closet and I immediately closed the door without picking them up.

"Here," I said to Sarah. "I've been writing, rewriting, polishing, crafting, working my little fingers to the bone. Here's one for you. It's my decision to come out of seclusion. Don't open it here. Save it for when you get home. Read it and you can think of me." I wondered if I existed to her if I wasn't around her. "What is it?" she asked.

"It's a poem. Do you like poetry?" I asked, as her face lit up to look at the envelope. She put it in her purse and poured some Jack Daniel's for both of us.

Then we had a discussion comparing poetry to lyrics. We both wondered if the lyrics of musicians were true—if the stories and accounts of relationships in songs were true. How were we to know? I know the accounts of my poetry were true, at the time. Love fades, love goes away, and then love returns to replace the love that went missing. As soon as love walks out of your life, love sidles in like it owns the joint—which is exactly how I walked into the diner this morning. I was proud of myself because Carly called me up and asked me to come drink wine with her in her hot tub yesterday. She has a great body to look at in a one-piece bathing suit. She's got some vicious curves in all the right places. So, this morning none of the retired men at the diner noticed my pride was high, but it was beaming. I wasn't quite in the clouds like I'd been laid, but it was good enough.

Typically, I have sex with Carly when she calls me to meet her at night, but she had to be up early the next day, and our tendency is to spend so much time at the act, morning and night, that neither of us wants to get out of bed in the morning. I couldn't put her in that predicament so I ducked out after four glasses of Chardonnay. At the same rate, I had just finished a seven-hour shift at the coffee shop, and I was probably a little too tired to manoeuvre the way she'd been accustomed to.

I've really learned a lot about how to be good in bed from Carly. It's useless knowledge, because I'd rather know how to love properly. Everyone has different preferences though. But it's important to know that after it's all said and done, win, lose, or draw at love, the afterimage of the sex remains vivid—more vivid than many of the other memories—still, the sex wasn't the love. When you really go back and analyse the moments that came before and after the sex, and you draw meaning from them, you realize how insignificant the sexual acts were to it all.

It's actually terribly sad that I don't remember much of our conversations because I was drunk, and because I had no thought that our relationship would end, I took the bulk of it for granted.

However, there was meaning in giving Sarah my poem.

After reading it, maybe more than once, she came back the next Friday, the day before Valentine's Day. She sidled in my door as if she owned the place that day, or I should say, in a manner drawing attention to the partially drank bottle of Jack Daniel's she had in hand. "Time to get jacked while we lounge around!" she said with a huge grin. Her visits with Jack Daniel's were becoming a tradition.

She sat on my bed, and immediately poured me a glass. She brought up the poem, talking about it in a way that made it seem insignificant to her. She did wonder if it was true, and she asked if it was written for her. I couldn't tell her the truth about the poem. It wasn't written for her, but I had come all that way into the plan of writing a book, yet all that way with her, and there was no turning back on the mission, or her. I was no longer on the same page I was writing.

And after I had had a few drinks and we had been lain together, relaxing as the drinks collected dust on my night table, she turned to me so that her face was just a few inches from mine. "I think you should come out of your prison sentence. You've done nothing to deserve this hell," she said. She paused for a moment, waiting for me to respond but I said nothing. "I don't think I can wait any longer," she said. I didn't know what she was waiting for, so I asked her just that.

She responded by kissing me on the cheek. I remained silent as she continued to kiss me and slowly work her wandering hands over my body. She climbed on top of me. "We don't have to wait," I said. "Do you have anything?" she asked. I reached into my night table, and took out one of the condoms and handed it to her. "Is this what you mean?" I said.

She took off her dress as she sat atop me. I undid my belt

and helped her remove my pants. I was already ready for her so she could put the condom on me. She got above me and slid all the way down to the bottom of the hilt. She emoted a feeling of pleasure, and as she made an O with her lips, I saw a ring of air come out of her mouth.

If you've ever wondered how to blow an O with air, it's the same as blowing an O with the smoke from a cigarette. First you inhale air or smoke, then you shape your lips into an O and blow a quick, strong exhalation from the back of your throat and out comes an O.

As she galloped and writhed slowly and passionately on me, I saw a taco with lettuce and sauce secrete out from underneath her pubis, becoming larger as it spiralled around, above her head in the shape of the golden ratio, slowly disappearing into her heart. I wiped some of the sauce that dripped onto my stomach and licked it off of my fingers. I was struggling to maintain my sanity in that moment. I'm not sure if my clarity of mind was lost because I was so excited to capitulate my love, or because I hadn't taken my Paliperidone injection in well over two months.

The sounds that she exhaled so passionately, I will never forget. To this day, I often remember, with great fervour, her amorous sounds while I'm by myself.

"Is this your first time?" she asked. I didn't respond because I was close to climax and she was so beautiful to see and hear, I couldn't interrupt it. I thought, *What if it's not your first time until you have had an orgasm during sex*? It was true that I had never had an orgasm during sex before. I climaxed then, as easily as falling down onto your head.

"Now it is," I said.

I didn't lose my erection right away so she took the condom off, looked at the juices inside it, and she sucked on me for a few minutes. I squirmed a bit with her lips on my sensitive post-climactic glans, and then she slowly caressed me, kissing my chest and making her way up to my lips to kiss me one last time before rolling over beside me, onto the bed.

Speechless, we paused for seemingly decades.

Then I laughed.

Then she laughed with me.

It's hard to say all of that was completely meaningless. I mark that it is similar to the first time you see an acquaintance in a long time—you've maybe only spoken once, briefly, barely been introduced, and the gesture to continue being acquaintances is continued even though it would be easier just to forget about each other. And in that gesture of deciding to speak, an entire world of possibility is opened; for you can see friendship on the horizon beyond the boundary held by each other. That's all it is—not meaningless. Sex is another intangible boundary we have, and I was allowed beyond Sarah's gate for a short time, like looking at us together, miles into the horizon.

Chapter Nine

Sunday March 11, 2018

When I was a young boy, someone asked me, "What's your favourite colour?" It might have been my mother or my father, or a teacher, but I'm not certain who asked me first. The first time anyone asks you that, it's an amazing question, because awareness of colour is so innate to children, from even before the time that they learn to speak. Once you've reached the age where you've learned to speak, you've already seen too many colours. I'm studying art in college, and our teacher told us that humans are capable of perceiving over twelve million different colours. That's a lot.

My response to the question was infallibly *blue*. But upon making that decision, I had put all the other colours behind the colour blue. Blue was the best of them all to me. In actuality, there is no colour better than another. They are all equal, but different.

I kept seeing blue everywhere, like when you see a movie and then, for weeks, you see quotes from it or you keep hearing people talking about it. Your friend buys a grey Volkswagen Beetle, and then you keep seeing a grey Volkswagen Beetle everywhere. That's what happened to me after I declared blue was the best of all colours. Every time I looked up at the sky, lo and behold was the colour blue. Then I quickly changed my favourite colour to *red* so my favourite colour wasn't a cliché.

As you grow up, you realize that the colour of the sky isn't actually blue on its own accord. There are natural phenomena that pertain to the reason the sky is perceived as blue. For one, the majority of the earth is covered with water and some say the sky is partially a reflection of the bodies of water that cover the earth. But, at the same time, there are some that will tell you that water is particularly clear, so in fact, the water looks blue because the sky is blue. Well, which is it? I'm not really a scientist, but it seems to be that the balance between the great ether and bodies of water compromises in a promise to appear as though they are both blue.

Maybe I've examined that notion a little too much, but it brings a sense of awe to the colour blue—that it is the colour of compromise, on the grandest scale on earth. So, I struggled to choose such an obvious colour as my favourite for a long time. But yesterday, as I was sitting on the dry, March steps to my door, drinking from a blue and gold can of Löwenbräu beer, I looked up at the sky and it reminded me of a time I experienced while I was locked up in my room on Etherington. It's something I always seem to put in the back of my mind, and pops into my head at times when I can't really spend any time to ruminate about it, but yesterday afternoon I had a bit of time.

I remembered one night in my incarceration around the time when we gain an hour of daylight in the mornings (today was also Daylight Saving Time), I saw a flash of light through my window in the distance. It panned across the view from the window in my room and then moments later the light hovered in my window, beaming a wondrous red colour. I went over to look.

I saw what looked like a fox running in the distance. It was beaming with a red light. The fox ran and ran around in the park that my window looked onto at the back of that house on Etherington. Then soon after, the fox ran up to the fence that bordered my back yard. It was a wire fence so I was able to see the fox on the other side, but it wasn't a fox. I had been mistaken, it was a lynx. The little lynx stood there with its breath hovering over his or her face, looking at me, glowing like a hot little red and orange orb. At the same time as being scared, I felt like going into the park to touch it. It amazed me, but at the same time, I felt there was something more to that beautiful alien beast like some kind of message was being transmitted to me through its presence.

And that was the last poem I wrote—a poem about seeing the alien lynx.

I woke up in the morning, after writing that poem, and I didn't think about the sight, but rather how I had described it in the poem. It wasn't a message about Paula (which is how I rendered it for the book). The lynx was a message about Sarah.

Sarah visited on Fridays for the last two weeks of March and on the last day she visited before April came, she said, "Next Wednesday is the first of April. We should meet at the diner. You up for it?"

I was all for it. I had moved on from Paula, despite fudging the truth for the sake of my book, and wanted to be with Sarah, but I hadn't been out of the house in what felt like many years. I had spent the whole winter holed up, almost completely by myself. I suffered a slight fear of re-entry, so I didn't respond satisfactorily to Sarah. "I'll try to be there," I told her. It didn't seem good enough for her, and I admit, it probably wasn't, considering all she had done to prevent me from totally disconnecting.

So, as I sat there yesterday, I looked at that can of blue and gold lager, and I looked up at the sky. In my beer-drunk soul and hands, I held a little piece of the sky—the can was the same colour as the sky and the sun that beamed like a beacon onto me in the waning heat of the late afternoon. I remembered in that moment that my favourite colour was once blue. Then I got to thinking a little more...

I thought that in writing this story about Sarah and I, I've come to realize that I've loved her completely, and only her in my life. She is like the sky and I am like a body of water and together we form my favourite colour—together we are blue—we are the promise of compromise and balance on a grand scale. For the first time in over two decades, my favourite colour is blue. It is my favourite again, in part, a declaration; and in part, an amendment. I've come back to her as if she was the only one that was meant for me, in my life.

I say that because I know what's next. I'm not quite sure I have the strength to go over what happened next, but I know that on the other side of that moment—definitive, to say the least—there is something good to look forward to. There is always something there for me, in what lies ahead, to get closer to Sarah wherever she is, and to get beyond the difficulties of some days.

For one, I still go to Ed's every day, and I'm slowly being accepted there by Randy and the other older men that make up the regulars. I went on my unicycle for the first few times this year. It's a lot quicker to get to the diner in the morning when I'm on the unicycle. I've stopped going to the lookout, and I don't think I'm going to bring that journey back into my routine. For now, I'm keeping my eyes open for a new place of solitude and solace that won't infringe on my intangible love for Sarah. Soon I will be with her in *our* place.

Chapter Ten

Saturday March 24, 2018

On the first of April, 2015, I was preparing my book to have a hard copy printed the next day. I didn't go to the diner to meet Sarah. I should have—something I regret not doing. In the early evening, I thought I finally finished preparing my document and was getting ready to go outside. I had no way to contact Sarah but if I liked what I felt, in the outside world, I would have certainly went to the diner to see her in the morning the next day. I was frightened by what it would be like to have my freedom back for the first time since the beginning of December, and I felt seeing Sarah would be too much for my baby steps back into society.

The first thing I wanted to do was use the bathroom. I wanted to use a toilet and a shower again—which reminds me—I specifically asked Sarah to leave my door unlocked from the outside when she left on the previous Friday so I could get out. I was just about to leave my room when I heard a knock on my door. I thought it was Sarah so I told her to come in. The door opened and behind it was Paula. "Vic, I need your help," she started. I asked her what was going on.

"I have to go to Winnipeg again. My mom died. She had a heart attack a couple days ago. I just got my cheque and I need you to find out what bus I can take," she said.

"I'm very sorry to hear that Paula. Are you okay?"

"I'm fine. She smoked for like fifty years. That's why I'm trying to quit. You should too," she said. I hadn't had a cigarette since December.

"Let me just use the bathroom first and I'll come help you. Just wait here," I told her.

"Good, cuz you look like shit," she said.

I went to the bathroom and used the toilet. Even though, I had used the bathroom several times in my seclusion, only when I was drinking with Sarah, in some ways using the toilet felt foreign to me. I had become used to squatting on the sawn bottles of water in my closet for so long that I almost forgot the comfort of having an actual toilet, and when you're drunk you don't appreciate much. This may seem ridiculous, but toilets are actually wondrous things.

I was about to have a shower so I took off all of my clothes. I decided to look in the mirror. The first thing I noticed was the large beard. It wasn't that large because my facial hair grows rather slow in some areas, but I wasn't looking forward to shaving it off. Once a beard gets too long, it becomes very tiresome to shave it. I looked at my beard for only a couple of seconds until I noticed I had become relatively emaciated.

I looked terrible. I was beginning to feel faint. I quickly

got in the shower trying to make myself look better, hoping I would feel better. After I showered, I went back into my room. "What's that smell," Paula asked. I told her it was bleach on a large pile of my workout clothes that I hadn't washed in a few months. She had no idea I hadn't been out of my room since she was with Dan, the guy with the malamute. The sight of her made me feel ill. Feelings of disgust overwhelmed me.

"What's wrong," she said.

"I'm not feeling very well."

"Come lie down and take a break." She was sitting on the edge of my bed.

"I don't feel good," I told her, wishing not to get close to her.

"Come lie down."

I went to the bed and sat down on the bed. "It's okay, we'll just lay here. Everything's going to be alright," she said. I lay down but I didn't start to feel any better. She asked me why she hadn't seen me in a long time but I was unable to respond. To be honest, the hallucinations were quite interesting, but the sickness I felt in that moment was awful. It felt like her words were vibrating painfully against me, the walls were blurry, as was everything else in my room. I was struggling to keep my eyes open. "I think I might be having a stroke," I said.

"What should I do?" she asked, and began stroking my leg. I was only wearing underwear at the time. I don't remember what Paula was wearing as she lay beside me on my bed, but I suppose Paula may not have looked like someone Sarah wanted to see when she walked in my room with that final bottle of Jack Daniel's in her hand. "Who are you?" Paula said.

"*Who am I? Who are you?*" Sarah said. Sarah left almost

immediately. I could barely concentrate on what was going on, completely unfit to go after her. "I don't know why you say goodbye, I say hello," she said loudly, walking down the hallway to leave. Oh, how terrible that moment was. I wish I could say it got better. I don't remember much of that time in my room, because I passed out immediately after Sarah stormed out—but today—today I started my day in our old place, the diner—knowing that she is with me.

I woke up in the hospital with tubes attached to my hand and wires attached to my chest to monitor my heart. The nurses came in shortly after I woke. "Get some rest Vic. We want to know what happened when you get some strength back," the one nurse told me. I was feeling better and my eyesight was normal. I was able to walk to stand at the side of my bed in the morning but I couldn't really go anywhere because I was attached to the tubes. I felt like walking around because I had some energy. I think it was mostly energy to see Sarah.

The nurse asked me if I wanted them to get my parents. My parents came to visit me later the next day. They brought me trail mix with chocolate pieces in it. I had to go to the bathroom within a half hour of eating the entirety of the large package. My dad told me the doctor didn't know how long I'd be there, but that they thought I would need to remain in the psychiatric ward after my blood pressure, blood sugar, and iron levels were somewhat normal. My dad asked me what happened, but I didn't really respond to him. "You gotta take better care of yourself, my boy," my dad said.

I stayed in there for a couple of weeks. They didn't keep me attached to the tubes for very long because they wanted me to start eating regular food and getting my energy levels back up by walking around the unit. I wanted to see Sarah very badly. She left so abruptly, and I wished that she would have known that I was in the hospital, ill.

After about a month, they found a room for me in the psych ward. I was walking around the unit and eating three meals a day regularly. There was tea and Sanka any time I wanted. They had me back on my Paliperidone injections, and they increased the dosage a little bit. After a few months there I was feeling okay. I wasn't hallucinating while I was in there, and I had enough energy to do anything I wanted again.

The day I shaved my beard was a little odd. They wouldn't let me alone with a razor, so one of the male nurses had to accompany me into the bathroom while I shaved my beard. It felt like something out of *One Flew over the Cuckoo's Nest*. I had to resist the urge to make a joke about using the razor in some kind of suicidal effort because I thought a joke like that would have adverse consequences (I really wanted to get out of there to see Sarah), so I kept my mouth shut about it. The nurse just stood there without saying a word.

My parents visited a few times and brought me food each time. I was glad about the food they brought. I was digesting normally again, since I had been eating the hospital food. They served shepherd's pie, steak, hamburgers, sandwiches, soup, cereal—all kinds of things—a lot of food that I was too piss-poor to buy on my own, on a regular basis.

One night, I got to thinking about when I would get out of there, what I would do first. I remembered that the only money I had spent since December was my rent payments. My social assistance provided me a little bit of spending money besides my rent, so it was safe to say that when I got out of the hospital, I probably had close to two thousand dollars waiting for me, plus more cheques coming as long as I stayed in the hospital. I felt the whole effort wasn't a total loss in that respect.

I don't think they really wanted me to leave the hospital so soon, but I would have lost my place of residence if I didn't go home to give the landlord new cheques. The post-dated cheques that I had provided to the landlord were about to run out in August, so I was allowed to leave the hospital at the end of July. I wasn't planning to buy a pack of cigarettes, but it was the first thing I bought when I left the hospital.

When I got back home my room was cleared out and the doorknob was turned back around the right way. I had given my parents my keys to look after my place while I was in the hospital. I wonder what they thought of my urinals and potties when they saw them. Just imagine your parents went in your room and saw jugs of urine and feces. I don't know. They had left the bottles of Jack Daniel's in my closet. My father is the type of guy that likes to always get his money's worth on everything he does, so it's strange he didn't realize that those empty bottles had some value if returned. Each bottle had a return value of forty cents.

She had left fourteen bottles there. They were worth a total of five dollars and sixty cents, but it was more important to note that she had visited fourteen times from the last week of December until the end of March, or every Friday during that time period. She didn't bring a bottle the first week she came and I'm not sure if she brought one on the first of April but she definitely didn't leave one there that night. Remembering it, it seemed cloudy in my mind as to whether she was there as regularly as she was, and the remaining bottles proved her presence. I almost still don't believe it. Women start out forth-coming, but it never lasts. The whole thing with Sarah was a tryst from normalcy, as I said.

I started going to the diner to see if she would be there. I didn't ask about her, but actually, after a few visits to the restaurant for the same meal that Sarah used to order, Ed asked me about Sarah. "Sarah was a friend of yours, right?" he asked. I told him I was, and then he explained that he knew someone that might want to speak with me and he asked for my phone number. I was excited that it might be Sarah so I quickly wrote it down for him. I'm the type of person that doesn't like to pry or ask about things that are none of my business, so Ed didn't tell me what happened to Sarah and I felt it was none of my business to ask either.

The day after that, I got a phone call from a police offi-cer. He wanted to talk to me and said I wasn't in any trou-ble, but that it would help them out if I came down to the station. I wasn't really doing anything, so I went.

When I met with the officer, the first thing he asked me was, "You knew Sarah Samson, is that right?" I told him I knew her, and I hadn't yet put it into perspective that he referred to our friendship in the past tense.

"Yes, I do," I said.

"Can I ask where you were on April first?"

"Sarah came over that night. I was with my roommate, half-naked when Sarah came in my room and then Sarah left when she saw that."

"What time was that?"

"I think it was probably around 7:00 PM, but I'm not really sure."

"What did you do after Sarah left?"

"I felt ill at the time and I became unconscious and I woke up in the hospital later that night."

"You know, we have records of Sarah mentioning you to her friends that night. We just wanted to be sure you weren't with her."

"With her where? I haven't seen her since that day. I was in the hospital until just a couple weeks ago."

"At the time of death."

"Time of death? What the hell happened?"

"It's looking like an accident. We haven't completely ruled out foul play or self-infliction."

"What are you talking about? Where's Sarah?"

"I'm sorry Mr. Glatt, but Sarah is gone. She passed away on April first."

I suppose I stopped talking to the police officer after that. I was catatonic and crying. I think I just walked away from his desk after he explained that she fell from a roof at the college while intoxicated.

I guess they probably checked my alibi after that. Having a doctor's record for an alibi is probably as good an alibi as you can get.

Oh dear, it was a terrible thing to think about. It was difficult to hear, and is difficult to think about when I say it now.

I got out of the police station and I couldn't concentrate to get on a bus so I just ran. I ran to the college to the roof that I knew he was talking about. Sarah wasn't there. I was hoping she'd be there. I sat there on one of the shipping pallets until it got dark, then I walked home.

I just imagine her singing loudly on that roof, songs of pining, howling loudly, at the top of her lungs, at the last one to see her alive—the panoptical moon—until the surprise of the plummet came.

I went to Ed's for breakfast the next morning, out of routine. I didn't say anything to Ed, and to this day, he hasn't mentioned anything more about Sarah.

I have read her obituary. It says that Sarah had a brother and she was a rising star on the local stand-up comedy scene. She never told me that she was a comedian. I did tell her that she was funny several times. I wish I had told her she had a completely infectious personality that I used to miss in between our Friday meetings. I wish I could tell her I still miss her now.

Paula was gone. I never saw Paula again either. She strangely left the cover of a biography of The Doors, called *Riders of the Storm,* in her empty room. I looked in her room when I came back from the hospital and that's all that was left in there. I took it and tacked it on my wall. When I moved out of that house at the end of August, I left it in my room.

I moved to a house just down the street, still on Etherington Crescent. I met Mateo there. I showed him my book and told him what happened with Sarah, and that I didn't really love Paula, that I was in love with Sarah. He told me I should publish the book anyway. "Just think of the feeling you'll have when you see your name in print, my friend. You may never have the opportunity again," he told me. I'm not sure he even understood the poetry—considering his English wasn't great. Still, I thought he was right so in January of 2016 I published that book.

And then at the end of March that year, I went to a bar. I was just waiting for a bus and I needed a place to get out of the cold, so I had a quick beer. At that time, I don't think I would have been able to remember the last time I had been to a bar. I probably hadn't been to a bar in about seven or eight years. There was a singer performing there. When I walked in he was playing *Don't think twice it's alright,* by Bob Dylan. I met some guys at the bar there and we were having a good time, and I kept drinking with them until midnight.

One of the guys took me down the street to another bar just before last call. As soon as we walked in that bar, some woman walked up and gave me a compliment on my jacket. The guy I was with bought me some beers and by closing time, I had my arms around that woman and she wanted me to take her home. That woman was Carly. I woke up beside her in her bed on April Fool's Day. It was starting to become notorious that on the first of April something a little out of the ordinary happened.

I kept up a purely sexual relationship with Carly since then. I would have been her boyfriend but she said that I didn't make enough money for her to be serious with me. I got a job later on that year at the cosmetics factory, and I told Carly about the job, but it still wasn't good enough for her. It was frustrating, especially since things weren't going well in my new place. Mateo was sleeping on a mattress he took out of the street when he moved in and I was starting to notice bed bugs in my room.

Mateo denied the whole thing, but I was in a lease until the end of August so I had to put up with the disgusting insects biting me every night while I tried to sleep. Carly and I broke it off and got back together several times before August, and by the time I moved to a new place in September, I guess all of my things were already contaminated by bugs. The next place

I moved still had the bugs. I had to put all of my stuff into storage that winter and move back in with my parents. I had just graduated in August, and to celebrate, I was a thirty-three year old man living with his parents again. On top of that, I couldn't get to the factory from my parents' place, so I had to quit my job.

On the first of April last year, somebody bought the first copy of my book. It was another sick April Fool's joke. Since then, I've sold about ten copies.

I guess I wrote this whole bit about the death of Sarah, a little before April Fool's because I'm expecting that this year something mysteriously unexpected, but serendipitous, will happen again. Maybe I'll find a new spot that can be for Sarah and me. Who knows what it's going to be? I'm looking forward to it.

I've been waiting all winter for this nice weather we've been getting and it's too hard to think of anything terrible happening. I guess I'm a little superstitious.

Chapter Eleven

Wednesday April 4, 2018

"Vic!" some young lady at the bus station called out to me. I turned around, almost falling off of my unicycle. I carried it with me, walking over to her as she motioned for me to come over. "You're Sarah's friend, right?" she asked. It was the first time I'd heard that name in about two years. I didn't respond. "Sarah told me about you," she continued. There was a tall man about the same height as me standing with her, waiting for the bus. I continued to talk to the young lady.

I wasn't planning to take the unicycle with me that day because there was a path between the college and my old house on Etherington that I wanted to check out. I wondered if the mud had dried up on the path. It's been a yearly event that I check out the path to find out how long it would take the mud to dry. From about March until April the path is muddy. I still remember walking through it, when I lived on Etherington, gathering mud on my shoes before all of my spring classes.

However, I had left my unicycle at the front door when I came home the night before and I didn't feel like bringing it upstairs to my room when I left on April Fool's Day. If I hadn't taken my unicycle, Sarah's friend would have been long gone, on her way to Burk's Falls by the time I arrived at the bus station downtown that day. It was a stroke of luck.

"Do you miss her?" she asked me.

"I think about her all the time. I'm not so sure I was very good to her."

"That's how people are."

"I just wish I had…"

"Some closure?"

"That's not what I was going to say, but now that you mention it…"

"We all do. She just left. She showed me pictures of you and she talked about you."

I don't know if it's a character flaw or a thing of politeness, but because I don't like to pry, I didn't ask what Sarah said about me. She seemed like she was hoping I would, but as moments like this have happened several times in my life, I also let that moment pass and we went along without mentioning the details.

"It's just hard to go on. I don't know if this is appropriate to say about her now, but I think I was in love with her," I said

"She said the same about you. She had trouble expressing her thoughts about guys and she never really said it. Outside all of the jokes she made, I knew her, and I knew she had strong feelings for you," she admitted. I started to well up with tears. I tried to hold it back but I let out a snotty snort. "Sorry," I said.

"It's okay, I know how you feel."

I asked her where she was going after that. She was in a line for the greyhound to North Bay. She was going to Burk's Falls though, one of the stops on the way up to Northern Ontario. She said she moved there about a year ago and that she missed being here.

I left the bus stop before she got on the bus, but seeing her that day was like something out of a dream. I never thought I'd hear about Sarah again. After meeting Sarah's friend, it felt like a message to me, directly from Sarah, like a piece of the closure I was looking for. In that moment I felt as connected to Sarah as I do to my distanced relationship with Adam Percy, the electrician-turned-monk. It seems I keep an air of far-reaching, almost unfathomably border-crossing love for people. They go away and they still feel my heart beating for them.

Sure, Adam is alive—I just hadn't heard from him in a long time. The day after I met Sarah's friend, Adam Percy showed up at my door. Well, a huge chunk of him did anyway. The manuscript for his first book arrived at my door with the accompanying letter asking if I would *please* edit it. He had been proud of me, and impressed by my literary work that he thought of me to edit his opus.

I sent him a letter later on in the day explaining that I would try to edit it. I was a little skeptical about being the man for the job, since his book is titled *The Joyous Fury and Fervour of Love*. I'm not certain I know anything about love, or if I can add anything of value to the content. Surely, Adam sees something in me that I'm not aware of. Hopefully this ignorance is only another one of my character flaws—for the sake of editing his book. But, I also told him I was interested to read it because I thought I might learn something.

So, it was the second of April on the Monday that I received Adam's book, almost as if the sacredness of April Fool's had extended beyond only one day. It felt like I was being rewarded for everything I've accomplished, in coming clean about my time with Sarah, throughout this winter. Who could expect as much wonder from life in two days?

The next day, yesterday, I was going to the diner in the morning. There was a notice on the door that read: *Closed today due to Family Emergency. We will be open again on Wednesday April 4.* I went to Tim Horton's for breakfast instead. I had a class in the afternoon and was planning to walk to the college after.

When I arrived at Tim Horton's there was a long line. Right in front of me in line was a pretty lady about my age, motioning to her dog through the window. The dog was excited, jumping up, unable to move very far because he was tied up with his leash. "I can't come, I'm tied up," I said to her, implying those were the dogs thoughts. "He hasn't had a bath in a while. He stinks. You don't want him in here right now," she said.

There was a commotion between one of the Tim Horton's managers and the workers. It was noticeable that the manager was upset with some of the workers. The last customer left in a tiff, dropping some napkins on the floor in front of myself and the lady with the dog. The two of us looked at each other and it was unspoken but understood, between the two of us, that the napkins should be picked up by one of us. I picked them up. The lady with the dog got her order and left. I just ordered a coffee and that wasn't unusual but something was calling me to this lady in the line.

I was holding the napkins so I went out of my way to the garbage can outside Tim Horton's to throw them out. That's where the lady had tied up her dog. If I didn't pick up the napkins, I wouldn't have walked over towards that lady. The lady started telling me that she had just left her job because her boss was nasty to her, and didn't treat her with respect, mentioning that the manager at Tim Horton's had just displayed similar actions moments before.

We continued talking for almost a half an hour after introducing ourselves. She told me her name was Virginia. I asked her where she was going. Her house was along the way to the college so I asked if I could walk her home. As we walked, she told me her dog was some sort of Labrador mix, but had a few health problems. I petted him because he was cute, but she reminded me again that he was very smelly, that I shouldn't have done that.

I told her I was a writer, which then led us into a conversation about philosophy. She mentioned that she was interested in the writings of Joseph Campbell. I wasn't sure who that was but she suggested some of his books to me. We got along very well, like long lost friends. She turned to me and said, "I want to give you my number." I took her number and I told her that I would send her some messages soon.

As we were about to part, at her apartment, we were in the middle of discussing that we felt there was something calling us to be together that day. "This is a relationship," she said to me. "Yes, I suppose it is," I said. And by that definition we were friends, accepting each other into each others lives. I was ecstatic after Virginia went home yesterday. I could barely concentrate in my manic state while in my class.

Actually though, we haven't made plans to meet. I feel more interested to see if I run into her somewhere in happenstance. I feel that, since we came together the first time that way, it would be better if we kept the relationship on that level—a spiritual level of connection that brings us together. Besides, I can always just take my unicycle through her neighbourhood a little more than I usually would. She did tell me she spends a lot of time in the park near her house. I like it there too.

As far as I know, that was the end of the magic of the beginning of April for me. Maybe there's more to come today. Who knows?

Chapter Twelve

Wednesday May 2, 2018

The wind is low, the birds will sing, and all that ...

I woke up early for work today—ten hours early—two hours before the diner was to open at five in the morning. I made a new playlist in the dark dawn then walked around my neighbourhood—the neighbourhood where this story all began. I listened to *Revolution 1* by The Beatles and could hardly withhold my inclination to walk to it in a joyous lilt along Etherington, appreciative of the wonderful May weather.

The energy that I had this morning was not just mine. There was something calling me out to move with it. And as the light opened up on the horizon above the blooming spring verdancy, I went to the diner as has been customary since my fourteenth and first graduating year of college.

After breakfast, I went to Virginia's favourite park near

her home. I waited there and waited some more, listening to my new playlist. She didn't come. However, when I sat on the bench in the park, I saw a beetle beside me, and although it was ugly, it was representative of freedom and nature, and beautiful at that. It pleased me for a moment then flew away.

I walked toward the lookout and as I was walking past a little elementary school at the top of the hill, a woman motioned for me to come over. At first, I didn't recognize her, but I soon realized it was Virginia. She had been taking her son to school that morning. "What are you doing here?" she asked. I told her I was listening to The Beatles, as she stroked the top of her son's head, just above her waist. "Aaron loves The Beatles, doesn't he?" she said.

"I believe it. How can you constrain your gait when walking and listening to *Revolution 1?*" I joked. Virginia looked at my face in disbelief. "What's your favourite album?" I asked.

Virginia sent Aaron off to school after she answered my question for him. She turned me around after that and I walked her back towards her apartment.

She discussed how she started a new job. I started to feel like she is inclined to dislike any kind of authority because she mentioned that she could not condone some of the unruly behaviour her new managers were permitting—sexual behaviour. Then she told me that she feels she gives off a sexual energy to people because they often tell her their sexual stories a little more candidly than she would like. But, she dropped a massive bomb of peace over us after that, even though she might never know how peaceful it was.

She told me Aaron is a fatherless child. Or, that is to say, he had a father, but he killed himself when Aaron was very young. Virginia felt that because her husband had left her by herself, it made her vulnerable to single men. She went on to explain that she had no intentions of pursuing, and frankly thinking about, a sexual relationship with any man because she was fully and completely devoted to her son's deceased father. In that moment I realized how we had been connected to one another due to a cosmic synchronicity—a certain necessary tangible life experience opened up from the potent womb of life's meaning.

That is to say, I had been pondering the thought that Sarah was the be all, end all love for me, that there should be no reason to look for any other. For one, the manner of the moments before her death point to the notion that it happened out of love—a love she had for me. But also, meeting Virginia, and witnessing her express her natural and, in fact, living love for a dead man, makes me feel that no other thing (person, or other) could ever bring me as close to fully loving Sarah like Virginia did today.

Hoping that my relationship with Virginia will continue to foster my love for Sarah, although I ignored mentioning it to her, I delightfully look forward to seeing her again, to always bring me closer to my love. Virginia and I are on the same spiritual road and completely apart, thankfully, tangibly together, and there is a certain beauty to how that is wonderful for both of us. I hope one day I am able to explain it to Virginia too.

I went to work after I parted with Virginia today. As I walked home from work, a gust of wind pushed me from behind, towards home. And now that I am home, I have arrived to where the world opened up and sent me—to a place I love being, where it makes sense to be, despite it being an infallibly imperfect place.

Check out Michael Whone's Novella, *Winter Lyric (2017)*

Proof

Made in the USA
Columbia, SC
07 June 2018